KU-519-944

"What are we running from?"

"Danger."

Ayme threw her hands up. "All I did was hop on a plane and come to England looking for Cici's father. How did that put me in danger?"

"It hasn't, exactly. It's put *me* in danger. And, because you're currently attached to me, it's put you in danger, too."

"Then maybe I should unattach myself."

The thought of "unattaching" from him filled her with dread. She didn't have a clue what she would do without him. And she really didn't want to find out.

"Maybe you should."

"On the other hand," she said, "if you would just let me know what's going on so I could be prepared, it would be nice."

He looked into her eyes. He was taking a risk in telling her. But what the hell? Life *was* a risk. And, despite everything, his gut feeling was that he could trust her.

Dear Reader

Have you ever been to the small, isolated island nation of Ambria?

Probably not. Few have. It's said to have white sand beaches as wide as those in the Caribbean, ocean-view hillsides like you see in Greece, food as exquisite as you find in France, towns as storybook-cute as Holland. The weather rivals Santa Barbara, the inhabitants are as welcoming as the South Pacific, the women all look like Sophia Loren and the men are clones of Cary Grant.

Sound good to you? My characters love it too—even though most have never been there either. But they've seen pictures, heard stories, and a few have even stood on the coast and caught sight of it out there in the Atlantic, playing peek-a-boo behind ocean clouds and rainbows.

It's funny, but finding a way to get out there, across those forbidding waters, braving the well-armed guards who patrol the rocky cliffs to keep out strangers, has become an obsession with many who were exiled when the current despot took over. They want their wonderful island country back, and they are plotting, even now, to have their way.

Want to go along? Come on. You've got nothing to lose but your heart.

Regards!

Raye Morgan

***Don't miss the second and third books
in this wonderful royal trilogy
The Lost Princes of Ambria
Coming soon!***

SECRET PRINCE,
INSTANT DADDY!

BY
RAYE MORGAN

MILLS & BOON

All the characters in this book have no existence outside the imagination of the author, and have no relation whatsoever to anyone bearing the same name or names. They are not even distantly inspired by any individual known or unknown to the author, and all the incidents are pure invention.

All Rights Reserved including the right of reproduction in whole or in part in any form. This edition is published by arrangement with Harlequin Enterprises II BV/S.à.r.l. The text of this publication or any part thereof may not be reproduced or transmitted in any form or by any means, electronic or mechanical, including photocopying, recording, storage in an information retrieval system, or otherwise, without the written permission of the publisher.

® and TM are trademarks owned and used by the trademark owner and/or its licensee. Trademarks marked with ® are registered with the United Kingdom Patent Office and/or the Office for Harmonisation in the Internal Market and in other countries.

First published in Great Britain 2010
Harlequin Mills & Boon Limited,
Eton House, 18-24 Paradise Road, Richmond, Surrey TW9 1SR

© Helen Conrad 2010

ISBN: 978 0 263 21440 6

Harlequin Mills & Boon policy is to use papers that are natural, renewable and recyclable products and made from wood grown in sustainable forests. The logging and manufacturing process conform to the legal environmental regulations of the country of origin.

Printed and bound in Great Britain
by CPI Antony Rowe, Chippenham, Wiltshire

Raye Morgan has been a nursery school teacher, a travel agent, a clerk and a business editor, but her best job ever has been writing romances—and fostering romance in her own family at the same time. Current score: two boys married, two more to go. Raye has published over seventy romances, and claims to have many more waiting in the wings. She lives in Southern California, with her husband and whichever son happens to be staying at home at that moment.

*This book is dedicated to Ineke
and all my Dutch cousins.*

CHAPTER ONE

PRINCE DARIUS MARTEN CONSTANTIJN of the Royal House of Ambria, presently deposed and clandestinely living under the name of David Dykstra, was not a heavy sleeper. Ordinarily the slightest unusual sound would have sent him slipping silently through his luxury penthouse apartment with a lethal weapon in hand, ready to defend his privacy—and his life.

The sense that his life might be under threat was not outrageous. Since he was a member of an overthrown monarchy, his very existence was a constant challenge to the thuglike regime that now controlled his country. And as such, he had to consider himself in constant jeopardy.

But tonight the instinct to defend his territory had been muted a bit. He'd hosted a cocktail party for fifteen rowdy London socialites and they'd all stayed much too long. That had a consequence he didn't suffer from often anymore, but its effects were not unfamiliar to him. He'd had too much to drink.

So when he heard the baby cry, he thought at first that he must be hallucinating.

"Babies," he muttered to himself, waiting to make sure the room had stopped spinning before he risked opening his eyes. "Why can't they keep their problems to themselves?"

The crying stopped abruptly, but by now he was fully awake. He listened, hard. It had to have been be a dream. There was no baby here. There couldn't be. This was an adult building. He was sure of it.

"No babies allowed," he murmured, closing his eyes and starting to drift back to sleep. *"Verboten."*

But his eyes shot open as he heard the little rule breaker again. This time it was just a whimper, but it was for real. No dream.

Still, in his groggy state, it took time to put all the pieces of this mystery together. And it still didn't make sense. There was no way a baby could be in his apartment. If one of his evening guests had brought one along, surely he would have noticed. And if this same ill-mannered person had left that baby behind in the coat room, wouldn't they have come back for it by now?

He tried to shrug the whole thing off and return to peaceful slumber, but by now, that was impossible. His mind was just awake enough to go into worry mode. He'd never go back to sleep until he was sure he was in a baby-free abode.

He groaned, then rolled out of bed, pulled on a pair of jeans he found in a pile on his chair and began to stalk quietly through his set of rooms, checking one after another and wondering grumpily why he'd leased a place with so many rooms, anyway. The living room was littered with cocktail napkins and empty crystal wine goblets. He'd sent the catering crew home at midnight—a mistake, he now realized. But who knew his party guests would stay until almost 3:00 a.m? Never mind, the cleaning lady would arrive in just a few hours and make everything clean and sparkling again.

"No more parties," he promised himself as he turned back to his search, kicking a long feather boa someone had left behind out of the way. "I'll just go to shindigs at other people's homes. I can still maintain my information sources and let others deal with the hassle."

But for now he had an apartment to search before he could get back to bed. He trudged on.

And then he found the baby.

It was asleep when he first saw it. He opened the door to his seldom-used media room and there it was, tucked into a drawer that was serving as a makeshift crib. The little mouth was open, the little round cheeks puffing a bit with each breath. It looked like a cute kid, but he'd never seen it before in his life.

As he watched, it gave an involuntary jump, its chubby little arms lurching upward, then falling slowly back again. But it didn't wake. Dressed in a pink stretch jumper that looked a little rumpled and a lot spit up on, the child seemed comfortable enough for now. Sleeping babies weren't so bad. But he knew very well what happened when they woke up and he shuddered to think of it.

It was pretty annoying, finding an uninvited baby in your home and it was pretty obvious who was to blame—the long, leggy blonde draped rather gracelessly across his cantilevered couch. He'd never seen *her* before, either.

"What in blazes is going on here?" he said softly.

Neither of them stirred, but he hadn't meant to wake them yet. He needed another moment or two to take in this situation, analyze it and make some clear-headed

decisions. All his instincts for survival were coming
alert. He was fairly certain that this was no ordinary
sleepover he'd been saddled with. This must have something to do with his royal past with its messy rebellion
history and his precariously uncertain future.

Worse, he had a pretty strong feeling it was going to
turn out to be a threat—maybe even the threat he'd been
expecting for most of his life.

He was fully awake now. He had to think fast and
make sound judgments. His gaze slid over the blonde,
and despite his suspicions about her, his immediate reaction was a light frisson of attraction. Though her legs
were sprawled awkwardly, reminding him of a young
colt who hadn't got its bearings right just yet, they were
shapely legs, and her short skirt had hitched up enticing-
ly as she slept, showing the aforementioned legs off in a
very charming way. Despite everything, he approved.

Most of her face was hidden by a mass of wiry curls,
though one tiny, shell-like ear peeked through, and she'd
wrapped her torso up tightly in a thick brown sweater.
She wasn't really all that young, but her casual pose
made her seem that way and something about her was
endearing at first glance. There was an appeal to the
woman that might have made him smile under other
circumstances.

But he frowned instead and his gaze snapped back to
stare at that gorgeous little ear. It was decorated with a
penny-sized earring that seemed familiar. As he looked
more closely, he could see it was molded in the form of
the old Ambrian coat of arms—the coat of arms of the
deposed royal family he belonged to.

As adrenaline shot through his system, his heart
began to thump in his chest and he wished he'd picked

up the weapon he usually carried at night. Only a very select set of people in the world knew about his connection to Ambria, and his life depended on it being kept a secret.

Who the hell was this?

He was pretty sure he was about to find out.

"Hey. Wake up."

Ayme Negri Sommers snuggled down deeper into her place on the couch and tried to ignore the hand shaking her shoulder. Every molecule of her body was resisting the wake-up call. After the last two days she'd had, sleep was the only thing that would save her.

"Come on," the shaker said gruffly. "I've got some questions that need some answers."

"Later," she muttered, hoping he'd go away. "Please, later."

"Now." He shook her shoulder again. "Are you listening to me?"

Ayme heard him just fine, but her eyes wouldn't open. Scrunching up her face, she groaned. "Is it morning yet?" she asked plaintively.

"Who are you?" the man demanded, ignoring her question. "What are you doing here?"

He wasn't going away. She would have to talk to him and she dreaded it. Her eyelids felt like sandpaper and she wasn't even sure they would open when she asked them to. But somehow she managed. Wincing at the light shafting in through the open door, she peered up through her wild hair at the angry-looking man standing over her.

"If you could give me just one more hour of sleep, we might be able to discuss this in a rational manner," she proposed hopefully, her speech slightly slurred. "I'm so tired, I'm hardly human at the moment."

Of course, that was a lie. She was human alright, and despite how rotten she felt, she was having a reaction to this man that was not only typically human, it was also definitely feminine. Bottom line, she was responding to the fact that he was ridiculously attractive. She took in the dark, silky hair that fell in an engaging screen over his forehead, the piercing blue eyes, the wide shoulders and the bare chest with its chiseled muscles, and she pulled in a quick little gasp of a breath.

Wow.

She'd seen him earlier, but from a distance and more fully clothed. Up close and half-naked was better. She recommended it, and under other circumstances she would have been smiling by now.

But this wasn't a smiling situation. She was going to have to explain to him what she was doing here and that wasn't going to be easy. She did try to sit up and made an unconvincing attempt at controlling her unruly hair with both hands. And all the while she was trying to think of a good way to broach the subject that she'd come for. She had a feeling it wouldn't be a popular topic. She would have to introduce it just right and hope for the best.

"You can do all the sleeping you want once we get you to wherever it is that you belong," he was saying icily. "And that sure as hell isn't here."

"That's where you're wrong," she said sadly. "I'm here for a reason. Unfortunately."

Little baby Cici murmured in her sleep and they both froze, staring at her for a moment, full of dread. But she sank back into deep slumber and Ayme sighed with relief.

"If you wake the baby up, you're going to have to take care of her," she warned him in a hushed voice. "I'm in a zombie trance."

He was sputtering. At least that was what it sounded like to her, but she wasn't in good judging form at the moment. He could have been swearing under his breath. Yes, that was probably it. At any rate, he wasn't pleased.

She sighed, shoulders sagging. "Look, I know you're not in the best shape yourself. I saw you when we first got here. You had obviously been enjoying your party a little too much. That's why I didn't bother to try to talk to you at the time. You know very well that you could use more sleep as much as I could." She scrunched up her nose and looked at him hopefully. "Let's call a truce for now and…"

"No."

She sighed, letting her head fall back. "No?"

"No."

She made a face. "Oh, all right. If you insist. But I warn you, I can barely put a sentence together. I'm incoherent. I haven't had any real sleep for days."

He was unrelenting, standing over her with strong hands set on his very tight and slender hips. The worn jeans rode low on them, exposing a flat, muscular stomach and the sexiest belly button she'd ever seen. She stared at it, hoping to deflect his impatience.

It didn't work.

"Your sleep habits are none of my concern," he said coldly. "I'm not interested. I just want you out of here and on your way back to wherever you came from."

"Sorry." She shook her head, still groggy. "That's

impossible. The flight we came on left for Zurich ages ago." She glanced at the baby, sleeping peacefully in the drawer. "She cried almost the whole trip. All the way from Texas." She looked up at him, expecting sympathy but not finding much. She made a face and searched his eyes, hoping for a little compassion at the very least. "Do you understand what that means?"

He was frowning like someone trying to figure all this out. "You flew here straight from Texas?"

"Well, not exactly. We did change planes in New York."

"Texas?" he repeated softly, as though he couldn't quite believe it.

"Texas," she repeated slowly, in case he was having trouble with the word itself. "You know, the Lone Star state. The big one, down by Mexico."

"I know where Texas is," he said impatiently.

"Good. We're a little touchy about that down home."

He shook his head, still puzzling over her. "You sound very much like an American," he said.

She shrugged and looked up with a genuine innocence. "Sure. What else would I be?"

He was staring at her earrings. She reached up and touched one of them, not sure what his interest was. They were all she had left from her birth mother and she wore them all the time. She knew her original parents had come from the tiny island country of Ambria. So had her adoptive family, but that was years ago and far away. Ambria and its problems had only been minimally relevant to her life as yet.

But then, she was forgetting that the Ambrian connection was the reason she was here. So naturally he would notice. Still, something about the intensity of his interest made her uncomfortable. It was probably safer to go back to talking about Cici.

"But as I was saying, she wasn't happy about traveling, and she let everyone know it, all across the Atlantic." She groaned, remembering. "Everyone on that plane hated me. It was hell on earth. Why do people have babies, anyway?"

His eyes widened and one eyebrow rose dramatically. "I don't know. You tell me."

"Oh."

She gulped. That was a mistake. She groaned internally. She really couldn't afford to goof up like that. He'd assumed Cici was her baby, which was exactly what she wanted him to think, at least for now. She had to be more careful.

She wished she were a better actor, but even a professional performer might have trouble with this gig. After all she'd been through over the past week, she really ought to be in a straightjacket by now. Or at least a warm bath.

Just days before, she'd been a normal young first-year lawyer, working for a small law firm that specialized in immigration law. And then, suddenly, the world had all caved in on her. Things had happened, things she didn't dare think about if she was to keep her wits about her. Things she would have to deal with eventually, but not yet…not now.

Still, she was afraid that nothing would ever be sane again. She'd turned around and found herself in the middle of a nightmare, and suddenly she'd had very limited choice. She could give up and go to bed and pull the covers over her head for the duration—or she could try to take care of what was left of her family and get baby Cici to where she belonged.

The question was moot, of course. She was used to doing what was expected of her, doing the responsible thing. She'd quickly decided on the latter course and now here she was, single-mindedly following the path she'd set for herself.

Once her mission was accomplished she would breathe a sigh of relief, go back to Texas and try to pick up the pieces of her life. That would be the time for facing what had happened and deciding how in the world she was going to go on now that everything was gone. But until then, for the sake of this tiny life she was protecting, she had to maintain her strength and determination no matter how hard it got.

In the meantime, she knew she had to lie. It went against her nature. She was usually the type who was ready to give her life story to anyone with a friendly face. But she had to squelch that impulse, hold back her natural inclinations and lie.

It wasn't easy. It was a painful lie. She had to make the world around her believe that Cici was her baby. She hadn't been a lawyer for long, but she knew a thing or two and one of them was that she would put this whole plan in jeopardy if people knew Cici wasn't hers, and that she had no right to be dragging her around the world like this. Social workers would be called in. Bureaucrats would get involved. Cici would be taken away from her and who knew what awful things might happen then.

Despite everything, she already loved that little child. And even if she didn't she would have done just about anything for Samantha's baby.

"Well, you know what I mean," she amended a bit lamely.

"I don't really care what you mean," he said impatiently. "I want to know how you got in here. I want to know what you think you're doing here." His blue eyes darkened. "And most of all, I want you to go somewhere else."

She winced. She could hardly blame him. "Okay," she said, pulling herself up taller in the seat. "Let me try to explain."

Was that a sneer on his handsome face?

"I'm all ears."

She knew very well he was being sarcastic. He didn't seem to like her very much. That was too bad. Most people liked her on sight. She wasn't used to this sort of hostility. She sighed, too sleepy to do anything about it, and went back to contemplating his ears.

They were very nice and tight to the sides of his head. She admired them for a moment. Everything about this man was pretty fine, she had to admit. Too bad she always felt like a gangly, awkward teenager around men like this. She was tall; almost six feet, and she'd been that tall since puberty. Her high school years had been uncomfortable. She'd been taller than all the boys until her senior year. People told her she was willowy and beautiful now, but she still felt like that clumsy kid who towered over everyone.

"Okay."

She rose and began to pace restlessly. Where to begin? She'd thought this visit was going to be pretty straightforward, but now that she was here, it seemed much more complicated. The trouble was, she didn't know all the sorts of facts a man like this was going to want to know. She'd acted purely on instinct, grabbing Cici and heading for London on barely a moment's notice. Panic, she supposed. But under the circumstances, she had to think it was understandable. She'd done the only thing she could think of. And now here she was.

She closed her eyes and drew in a deep, shaky breath. She'd come to this man's apartment for a reason. What was it again? Oh, yes. Someone had told her he could help her find little Cici's father.

"Do you remember meeting a girl named Samantha?" she asked, her voice cracking a bit on the name. Now it was going to be a chore just to keep from crying. "Small, blonde, pretty face, wore a lot of jangly bracelets?"

He swayed just a little and looked to be about at the end of his tether. She noticed, with a bit of a start, that his hands were balled into tight fists at his side. Another moment or two and he was going to be tearing his hair out in frustration. Either that or giving her shoulders a firm shake. She took a step backward, just in case.

"No," he said, his voice low and just this side of angry. "Never heard of her." His brilliant blue eyes were glaring at her. "And never heard of you, either. Though you haven't provided your own name yet, so I really can't say that, can I?"

"Oh." She gave a start and presented herself before him again, chagrined that she'd been so remiss.

"Of course. I'm sorry." She stuck out her hand. "My name is Ayme Sommers. From Dallas, as if you couldn't tell."

He let her stand there with her hand out for a beat too long, still looking as though he couldn't believe this was happening. For a moment, she thought he was going to refuse to respond and the question of what she was going to do next flitted into her head. But she didn't have to come up with a good comeback, after all. He finally relented and slid his hand over hers, then held on to it, not letting her go.

"Interesting name," he said dryly, staring hard into her dark eyes. "Now tell me the rest."

She blinked at him, trying to pull her hand back and not getting much cooperation. She was suddenly aware of his warm skin and hard muscles in a way that stopped the breath in her throat. She tried not to look down at his chest. It took all her strength.

"What do you mean?" she said, her voice squeaking. "What 'rest'?"

He pulled her closer and she gaped at him, not sure why he was playing this game of intimidation.

"What is your tie to Ambria?" he asked, his voice low and intense.

She gasped, her eyes wide, and gazed at him in wonder. "How did you know?"

He inclined his head in her direction. "The Ambrian shield on your earrings pretty much gives it away."

"Oh." She'd forgotten. Her mind was full of cotton right now. It was amazing that she even remembered who she was. She touched one ear with her free hand. "Of course. Most people don't know what it is."

His eyes narrowed. "But you do."

"Oh, yes."

She smiled at him and he winced, and almost took a step backward himself. Her smile seemed to light up the room. It was too early for that—and inappropriate considering the circumstances. He had to look away, but he didn't let go of her hand.

"My parents were from Ambria. I was actually born there. My birth name is Ayme Negri."

That sounded like a typically Ambrian name, as far as he knew. But he didn't really know as much as he should. This girl with the shields decorating her ears might very well know a lot more than he did about his own country.

He stared at her, realizing with a stunned, sick feeling that his true knowledge of the land his family had ruled for a thousand years was woefully inadequate. He didn't know what to ask her. He didn't know enough to even conjure up a quick quiz to test her truthfulness. All these years he'd had to hide his identity, and in the process he hadn't really learned enough. He'd read books. He'd talked to people. He'd remembered things from his early childhood. And he'd had one very effective mentor. But it wasn't enough. He didn't know who he was at his very core, nor did he know much about the people he came from.

And now she'd arrived, a virtual pop quiz. And he hadn't studied.

Her hand in his felt warm. He searched her face. Her eyes were bright and questioning, her lips slightly parted as though waiting for what was going to happen next and slightly excited by it. She looked like a teenage girl waiting for her first kiss. He was beginning to think that the alarm, which had gone off like a whistle in his brain, was a false one.

But who was she really and why was she here? She seemed so open, so free. He couldn't detect a hint of guile in her. No assassin could have been this calm and innocent-looking.

It was pretty hard to believe that she could have been sent here to kill him.

CHAPTER TWO

"AYME NEGRI," he repeated softly. "I'm David Dykstra."

He watched her eyes as he said the name. Was there a slight blink? Did she know it was an alias?

No, there was nothing there. No hint of special knowledge. No clues at all. And it only made sense. If she'd wanted to finish him off, she'd had her chance while he was sleeping.

Still, he couldn't let his guard down. He'd been waiting for someone to arrive with murder on his mind since that dark, stormy night when he was six years old and he'd been spirited away from the rebellion in Ambria and across the countryside in search of a safe haven.

The palace had been burned and his parents killed. And most likely some of his siblings had died as well—though he didn't know for sure. But he'd been rescued and hidden with a family in the Netherlands, the Dykstras. He'd been spared.

All that had happened twenty-five years ago, and no one had ever come to find him, neither friend nor foe. Someday he knew he would have to face his destiny. But maybe not today.

"Ayme Negri," he said again, mulling over the name.

He was still holding her hand, almost as though he was hoping to gain some comprehension of her motives just by sense of touch.

An Ambrian woman, raised in Texas. That was a new one to him.

"Say something in Ambrian," he challenged quickly. At least he had a chance of understanding a little of the language if she didn't get too complicated. He hadn't spoken it since he was a child, but he still dreamed in his native tongue sometimes.

But it didn't seem she would be willing to go along with that little test. Her eyes widened and a hint of quick anger flashed across her face.

"No," she said firmly, her lovely chin rising. "I don't have to prove anything to you."

His head reared back. "Are you serious? You break into my apartment and now you're going to take on airs?"

"I didn't break in," she said indignantly. "I walked in, just like everybody else you had here to your party. I...I sort of melted into a group that was arriving and no one seemed to think twice."

She shrugged, remembering how she'd slipped into the elevator with a bunch of boisterous young city sophisticates. They seemed to accept her right to come in with them without a second thought. She'd smiled at a pretty young woman in a feathered boa and the woman had laughed.

"Look, she's brought a baby," she said to her escort, a handsome young man who had already had much too much to drink. "I wish I had a baby." She turned and pouted. "Jeremy, why won't you let me have a baby?"

"What the hell, babies for everyone," he'd called out

as the elevator doors opened, and he'd almost fallen over with the effort. "Come on. If we're going to be handing out babies, I'm going to need another drink."

Laughing, the group had swelled in through the door to this apartment and left her standing in the entryway. No one else had noticed her. She'd seen the host in the main room, dancing with a beautiful raven-haired woman and swaying like a man who'd either fallen in love or had too many rum drinks. She'd sighed and decided the better part of valor was to beat a hasty retreat. And that was when she'd slipped into the media room and found a drawer she could use as a bassinet for Cici.

"I don't remember inviting you," he noted dryly.

"I invited myself." Her chin lifted even higher. "Just because you didn't notice me at the time doesn't make me a criminal."

He was ready with a sharp retort, but he bit his tongue. This was getting him nowhere. He had to back off and start over again. If he was going to find out what was really going on, he needed to gain her trust. Making her defensive was counterproductive at best.

And he did want to know, not only because he was plain curious, but because of the Ambrian connection. There had to be a reason for it. Young Ambrian women weren't likely to just appear on his doorstep out of the blue. In fact, it had never happened before.

"Sorry," he said gruffly, turning away. Taking a deep breath and calming himself, he looked back and his gaze fell on the little child. There had been a period, while living in his huge adoptive family, when he'd spent a lot of time with babies. They didn't scare him.

Still, he could take or leave them. They were often just too much work.

But he knew very well what happened when one of this age was woken from a sound sleep, and the results were never very pretty.

"Listen, let's go to the kitchen and get a cup of coffee. Then we can talk without waking up your baby."

"Okay." She stopped, looking back. "Shall I just leave her here?" she asked doubtfully.

Cici had been practically glued to her body ever since Sam had left her behind that rainy Texas day that seemed so long ago now. And yet it hadn't even been a week yet. She smiled, suddenly enchanted with the way the child looked in the drawer.

"Look at the little angel. She's sleeping like a lamb now."

He frowned. "How old is that baby?" he asked suspiciously.

That was another question she wasn't confident enough to answer. Sam hadn't left behind any paperwork, not even a birth certificate.

"Her name's Cici," she said, stalling for time.

His glare wasn't friendly. "Nice name. Now, how old is she?"

"About six weeks," she said, trying to sound sure of herself and pretty much failing at it. "Maybe two months."

He stared at her. Skepticism was too mild a term for what his gaze was revealing about his thoughts on her answer.

She smiled brightly. "Hard to remember. Time flies."

"Right."

She followed him out into the living room. He snagged a shirt from the hall closet as they passed it, shrugged into it but left it open. She made an abrupt turn so he wouldn't find her staring at him, and as she did so, she caught sight of the view from the huge floor-to-ceiling picture window.

She gasped, walking toward it. It was four in the morning but the landscape was still alive with lights. Cars carried people home, a plane cruised past, lights blinking. Looking down, she was suddenly overwhelmed with a sense of detached wonder. There were so many people below, all with their own lives, going on with things as though everything was normal. But it wasn't normal. The world had tipped on its axis a few days ago. Nothing would ever be the same again. Didn't they know?

For just a moment, she was consumed with a longing to be one of those clueless people, riding through the night in a shiny car, going toward a future that didn't include as much heartbreak and tragedy as she knew was waiting for her once this adventure in Britain was over.

"Wow. You can see just about all of London from here, can't you?" She was practically pressing her nose to the glass.

"Not quite," he said, glancing out at the lights of the city. He liked this place better than most. It was close to the building where his offices were—centrally located and perfect for running the British branch of his foster father's multinational shipping business. "But it is a pretty spectacular view."

"I'll say." She was standing tall, both hands raised, fingertips pressed to the glass to hold her balance as she leaned forward, taking it all in. She looked almost poised to fly away over the city herself.

He started to suggest that she might want to keep her hands off the window, but as he watched her, he checked himself. With her long limbs and unusual way of holding her posture, she had an unselfconscious gawkiness, like a young girl, that was actually quite winsome. But she really wasn't all that young, and in that short skirt, her legs looked like they went on forever. So he kept quiet and enjoyed his own temporary view, until she tired of it and levered back away from the glass.

"Cities like this are kind of scary," she said, her tone almost whimsical. "You really get the feeling it's every man for himself."

He shrugged. "You're just not used to the place. It's unexplored territory to you." His wide mouth quirked. "As the song says, faces are ugly and people seem wicked."

She nodded as though pleased that he saw the connection. "That's the way I felt coming here tonight. A stranger in a very weird part of town."

He almost smiled but hadn't meant to. Didn't really want to. He needed to maintain an edgy sort of wariness with this woman. He still didn't know why she was here, and her reasons could be costly to him for all he knew.

Still, he found himself almost smiling. He bit it off quickly.

"This part of town is hardly weird," he said shortly. The real estate was high class and high-toned, and he was paying through the nose for that fact. "Maybe you miss the longhorns and Cadillacs."

She gave him a haughty look. She'd caught the ill-concealed snobbery in his tone. "I've been out of Texas before, you know," she said. "I spent a semester in Japan in my senior year."

"World traveler, are you?" he said wryly. But he rather regretted having been a little mean, and he turned away. He needed to be careful. The conversation had all the hallmarks of becoming too personal. He had to break it off. Time to get serious.

He led her on into his ultramodern, wide-open kitchen with its stainless-steel counters and green onyx walls. He got down two mugs, then put pods into the coffee machine, one at a time. In minutes it was ready and he handed her a steaming mug of coffee, then gazed at her levelly.

"Okay, let's have it."

She jumped in surprise. "What?" she asked, wide-eyed.

He searched her dark eyes. What he found there gave him a moment of unease. On the surface she seemed very open and almost naive, a carefree young woman ready to take on the world and go for whatever was out there. But her eyes held a more somber truth. There was tragedy in those eyes, fear, uncertainty. Whatever it was that she was hiding, he hoped it had nothing to do with him.

"Who are you and what are you doing here?" he asked again. "Why are you carrying around a very young baby in a strange city in the middle of the night? And most important, how did you even get in here?"

She stared at him for a moment, then tried to smile as she took a shallow sip of the hot coffee. "Wow. That's a lot to throw at a girl who's only half-awake," she noted evasively.

His grunt held no sympathy. "You threw a six-week-old baby at me," he reminded her. "So let's have it."

She took a deep breath, as though this really was an effort. "Okay. I think I already explained how I got in here. I hitched a ride with a party group and no one minded."

He groaned, thinking of some choice words he would have with the doorman later that day.

"As I told you, my name is Ayme Negri Sommers. I'm from Dallas, Texas. And…" She swallowed hard, then looked him in the eye. "And I'm looking for Cici's father."

That hit him like a fist in the stomach. He swallowed hard and searched her gaze again. He knew very well that he was now treading into a minefield and he had to watch his step very carefully.

"Oh, really?" he said, straining to maintain a light, casual tone. "So where did you lose him?"

She took it as a serious question. "That's just the trouble. I'm not really sure."

He stared at her. Was she joking? Nothing she said was making any sense.

"But I heard from a very reliable source," she went on, setting down her mug and putting her hands on her hips as she turned to look questioningly at him, "that you would be able to help me out."

Ah-ha. A very dangerous mine had appeared right in front of him with this one. Careful!

"Me?" he asked, trying not to let his voice rise with anxiety. "Why me?"

She started to say something, then stopped and looked down, uncomfortable and showing it. "See, this is why this is so hard. I don't really know. My source said that you would know where to find him." She looked back up into his face, waiting.

"So you think it's someone I know?" he asked, still at sea. "Obviously, it's not me."

She hesitated much too long over that one and he let out an exclamation, appalled. "You can't be serious. I think I would have noticed a little thing like that, and I know damn well I've never seen you before." He shook his head in disbelief.

She sighed. "I'm not accusing you of anything."

"Good. So why are you here?"

She took a deep breath. "Okay, the person who advised me to look you up is a man associated with the firm I work for."

"In Texas? And he thinks he knows who I know?" He shook his head, turning away and beginning to pace the floor in frustration. "This is absurd. How did he even know my name?"

"He told me you socialize in the same circles as Cici's dad. He said, 'Don't worry. He'll know how to find him.'"

"Oh, he did, did he?" For some reason this entire conversation was stoking a rage that was smoldering inside him. He stopped and confronted her. "So this person who's supposed to be Cici's father—this person I'm supposed to know where to find—what's his name?"

She half twisted away. This had all seemed so easy when she'd planned it out as she made her way to the airport in Dallas. She would dash off to London, find Cici's father, hand over the baby and head back home. She hadn't realized she would have to try to explain it all to someone in between. When you got right down to it, the bones of the story weren't making a lot of sense.

And she realized now that one element would sound really goofy to this man. She was hoping to keep that one under wraps for as long as possible.

She turned back with a heart-wrenching sigh and said dramatically, "Well…you see, that's the problem. I'm not sure what his actual name is."

He stared at her. The absurdity of the situation was becoming clear. She was looking for a man who had fathered her baby. She didn't know where he was. She didn't know his name. But she'd come here for help. And he was supposed to ride to the rescue? Why, exactly?

It was true that he had a reputation for knowing everyone who counted within a certain social strata. He'd made it his business to know them, for his own purposes. But he had to have something to go on. He couldn't just throw out possibilities.

"What are you going to do when you find him? Are you planning to marry the guy?"

"What?" She looked shocked, as though this very mundane idea was too exotic to contemplate. "No. Of course not."

"I see," he said, though he didn't.

She bit her lip and groaned silently. She was so tired. She couldn't think straight. She just wanted to go back to sleep. Maybe things would look clearer in the morning.

"How am I supposed to find someone if I don't know his name?"

She turned and gave him an exasperated look. "If this were easy, I could have done it on my own."

"I see. I'm your last resort, am I?"

She thought for a second, then nodded. "Pretty

much." She gazed at him earnestly, feeling weepy. "Do you think you can help me?"

He gazed at her, at her pretty face with those darkly smudged, sleepy eyes, at the mop of blond hair that settled wildly around her head as though it had been styled by gypsies, at her slightly trembling lower lip.

He had a small fantasy. In it, he told her flat out, "Hell, no. I'm not helping you. You give me nothing and ask for miracles. I've got better things to do with my time than to run all over London looking for someone I'm never going to find. This is insane."

As the fantasy began to fade, he saw himself reaching into his pocket and handing her money to go to a hotel. What a happy little dream it was.

But looking at her, he knew it wasn't going to happen. Right now, her eyes were filling with tears, as though she could read his mind and knew he wanted to get rid of her and her problems.

"Okay," he told her gruffly, clenching his fists to keep from following his instinct to reach out to comfort her. And then he added a touch of cynicism to his tone, just for good measure. "If all this is a little too overwhelming for you in your current state of hysteria…"

"I am not hysterical!" she cried indignantly.

He raised an eyebrow. "That's a matter of judgment and not even very relevant. Why don't we do this in a logical, methodical fashion? Then maybe we can get somewhere."

She moaned. "Like back to bed?" she suggested hopefully.

"Not yet." He was pacing again. "You need to fill in some of the blanks. Let's start with this. What exactly is your tie to Ambria? Give me the full story."

He'd given up wondering if she was here to harm him. The complete innocence she displayed wasn't very likely to be a put-on. And anyway, what sort of an incompetent murder master would send a young woman with a baby to do the dirty deed? It just didn't make sense.

"My parents were Ambrian," she began. "I was actually born there but that was just before the rebellion. My birth parents died in the fighting. I don't remember them at all. I was taken out with a lot of other refugee children and rushed to the States. I was adopted right away. I was only about eighteen months old, so as far as I'm concerned, my adoptive parents are my parents." She shrugged. "End of story."

"Are you kidding? We've barely begun." He stopped and looked down at her, arms folded over his chest. "Who told you about your Ambrian background?"

"Oh, the Sommerses had Ambrian roots, too. Second generation American, though. So they told me things, and there were some books around the house." She shook her head. "But it wasn't like I was immersed in the culture or anything like that."

"But you do know about the rebellion? You know about the Granvilli family and how they led an illegal coup that killed a lot of people and left them in charge of an ancient monarchy that should have been left alone?"

She blinked. "Uh...I guess."

"But you don't know much about it?"

She shook her head.

He gazed at her, speculation glowing in his silver-blue eyes. "So you don't have family still in Ambria?"

"Family?" She stared at him blankly. "Not that I know of."

"I guess they were all killed by the rebels?"

She blinked and shook her head. "I don't know if the rebels killed them."

He raised a cynical eyebrow. "Who do you think killed them?"

She ran her tongue nervously over her lower lip. "Well, to tell you the truth, I really don't know what side they were on."

That stunned him. The idea that someone decent might support the rebels who had killed his parents and taken over his country didn't really work for him. He dismissed it out of hand. But if she were around long enough, and he had a chance, he would find out who her parents were and what role they played. It seemed like something she ought to know.

"Now that we've established who you are, let's get to the real topic. Why are you really here?"

She sighed. "I told you."

But he was already shaking his head. "You told me a lot of nonsense. Do you really expect me to believe you had a baby and don't know the father? It doesn't add up, Ayme. How about giving me the real story?"

She felt like a bird caught in a trap. She hated lying. That was probably why she did it so badly. She had to tell him something. Something convincing. Had to be. She was beginning to see that she would really be in trouble if he refused to help her.

But before she could conjure up something good, a wail came from across the apartment. Ayme looked toward where the sound was coming from, uncertainty on her face. Why didn't this baby seem to want to sleep for more than an hour at a time, day or night?

"I just fed her an hour ago," she said, shaking her

head and thinking of her dwindling stash of formula bottles. "Do you think she really wants to eat again?"

"Of course," he told her. "They want to eat all the time. Surely you've noticed."

She bit her lip and looked at him. "But the book says four hours...."

He groaned. She was still using a book?

"Babies don't wear watches," he noted, feeling some sympathy for this new mother, but a lot of impatience, as well.

"True." She gave him a wry look as she turned to go. "But you'd think they could look at a clock now and then."

He grinned. He couldn't help it. If he really let himself go, he would start liking her and he knew it. And so he followed her into the room and watched as she stroked the little round head rather inefficiently. The baby was definitely crying, and the stroking was doing no good at all. From what he could tell, Ayme didn't seem to have a clue as to what to do to quiet her.

"Why don't you try changing her?" he suggested. "She's probably wet."

"You think so?" That seemed to be a new idea to her. "Okay, I'll try it."

She had a huge baby bag crammed full of things, but she didn't seem to know what she was looking for. He watched her rummage around in it for a few minutes, then stepped forward and pulled out a blanket which he spread out on the couch.

"I can do this," she said a bit defensively.

"I'm sure you can," he said. "I'm just trying to help."

She winced, feeling genuine regret for her tone. "I know. I'm sorry."

She pulled out a paper diaper and laid it on the blanket, then pulled Cici up out of the drawer.

"There you go little girl," she cooed to her. "We're going to get you nice and clean."

David stood back and watched, arms folded across his chest, mouth twisted cynically. She didn't seem very confident to him. Cici wasn't crying hard, only whimpering at this point, but he had the impression that she was looking up at the woman working over her with something close to apprehension.

"Don't you have someplace else you could be?" she muttered to him as she worked, and he could see that she was nervous to be doing this in front of him. Like someone who didn't really know what she was doing.

One thing he knew for sure—this woman didn't know the first thing about taking care of a baby. How crazy was that? And then it came to him. She wasn't the mother of the baby. Couldn't be. In six weeks time anyone would have learned more than she seemed to know.

"Alright Ayme Negri Sommers," he said firmly at last, "come clean. Whose baby is this?"

She looked up, a deer in the headlights.

"Mine."

"Liar."

She stared at him for a moment, degrees of uncertainty flashing across her pretty face. Finally, she threw her hands into the air. "Okay, you got me." She shrugged, looking defeated. "She's not really mine." She sighed. "What was your first clue?"

He grunted, stepping forward to take over. "The fact

that you don't know beans about taking care of a baby," he said, taking the diaper from her and beginning to do an expert job of it in her place. "The fact that you're still reading a book to figure out which end is up."

She heaved a heart-felt sigh. "I guess that was inevitable. It's really such a relief. I hated living a lie." She looked at him with more gratitude than resentment. "How come you know so much about babies, anyway?"

"I grew up in a big family. We all had to pitch in."

She sighed. "We didn't have any babies around while I was growing up. It was just me and Sam."

The baby was clean and in dry diapers. David put her up against his shoulder and she cuddled in, obviously comfortable as could be and happy to be with someone who knew what he was doing. He managed a reluctant smile. It was just like riding a bicycle. Once you knew how to hold a baby, you didn't forget.

He turned back to Ayme. "Who's this Sam you keep talking about?"

She swallowed, realizing the answer to that question was going to be tied to very different emotions from now on.

"My...my sister, Samantha. She was Cici's real mother."

And that was when the horror hit her for the first time since she'd left home. Her legs turned to rubber. Closing her eyes, she sank to the couch, fighting to hold back the blackness that threatened to overtake her whenever she let herself think, even for a moment, about Samantha. It was the same for her parents. The accident had taken them, too. Her whole family.

It was all too much to bear. If she let herself really

think about what had happened and about the emptiness that was waiting for her return to Dallas, the bubble she was living in would pop in an instant. She couldn't think about it and she couldn't tell him about it. Not yet. Maybe not ever. The pain was just too raw to manage.

Steeling herself, she forced out a quick explanation.

"Sam died in a car accident a few days ago." Her voice was shaking but she was going to get through this. "I...I was taking care of Cici when it happened. It was all so sudden. It…"

She took in a gasping breath, steadying herself. Then she cleared her throat and went on.

"Now I'm trying to get her to where she belongs. I'm trying to find her father." She looked up, surprised to find that she'd gone through it and was still coherent. "There. Now you know it all."

He stared at her. Her eyes looked like dark bruises marring her pretty face. The tragedy in her voice was mirrored by her body language, the tilt of her head, the pain in her voice. He didn't doubt for a minute that everything she'd just told him was absolutely true and it touched him in a way he hadn't expected.

The urge was strong to put down the baby and take the woman in his arms. If anyone needed a bit of comfort, Ayme did. But he stopped himself from making that move. He knew it wouldn't work out well. The last thing she wanted right now was compassion. The smallest hint of sympathy would very probably make her fall apart emotionally. He assumed that she didn't want that any more than he did. At least he hoped so. He looked away and grimaced.

But—back to basics—he still didn't understand why she'd come to him.

"Ayme, I'm not Cici's father," he said bluntly.

"Oh, I know. I know it's not you."

He shook his head, still at sea and searching for landfall. "Then why are you here?"

She shrugged. "You're going to help me find him." She gazed at him earnestly. "You just have to. And since you're Ambrian..."

"I never said I was Ambrian," he broke in quickly. He had to make that clear. As far as the rest of the world knew, he was a citizen of the Netherlands, born and bred Dutch. That was the way it had been for twenty-five years and that was the way it had to be.

"Well, you know a lot about Ambria, which not a lot of people do."

Reluctantly, he admitted it. "True."

Rising from the couch, she began to pace much the way he had a few minutes earlier. She was exhausted and her emotions were spent. But she had more work to do. Glancing over at David, she noticed that Cici's downy head was tucked against his shoulder and the little eyes were closed. She was asleep. Ayme's sigh was from the depths of her wounded soul.

"If only I'd had you along on the flight over the Atlantic," she said.

"Don't try to change the subject," he said, turning to lay the baby down very carefully in her makeshift bed. "If you want my help, you've got to give me more. I can't do anything unless I understand the parameters I'm dealing with."

She nodded. He was right, of course. But what could she say to explain this crazy situation? She moved restlessly toward the doorway and leaned against the doorjamb. From there, she could see across the living room and out through the huge picture window surveying the city. The mass of city lights spread out below added a manic energy, despite the time of night.

That made her think—what if all those lights went out one night?

She nodded, realizing that the stars would take their place. And that would be a whole different dynamic. She wasn't sure which she would prefer at the moment— manic energy or soothing starlight. But her preference didn't mean a thing. She had to deal with what she had before her.

Throwing her head back, she began.

"Sam didn't tell me much about Cici's father. Actually, I hadn't seen her for almost a year when she showed up with a baby in her arms. I had no idea…" She put a hand to her forehead as she remembered the shock of Sam's return home. "Anyway, she didn't tell me much, but she did tell me that Cici's father was Ambrian. That she'd met him on a trip to London. And that she wanted nothing more in the world at that moment than to find him and show him his baby."

Of course, there were other moments, even hours, when Sam acted as though she didn't care at all—espe- cially when she took off without her baby. But he didn't have to know about that.

She turned and came back into the room, watching David tuck a blanket in around Cici. It was unusual to see such a strong, handsome man doing something like that. At least it seemed unusual to her. But who knew? Maybe she should get out more.

That sweet little baby was finally getting the sort of care she deserved. She thought of how careless Sam had seemed with Cici. Their mother had been appalled.

But maybe that was because of her precarious circumstances. If she could have found Cici's father and they could have formed a real family, maybe things would have been different.

"Now she'll never get the chance," she murmured softly, then caught herself and frowned. None of that. She couldn't let herself drift off into that sort of sadness. They would never get anything done.

He'd finished with the baby and he came to stand in front of her, looking down. "But she didn't tell you this guy's name?"

She hesitated. "She told me a name, but...."

"Who? You've got to tell me, Ayme. I don't see how I can help you if you won't tell me."

She turned away again and he followed her out to the picture window. "Do you ever see the stars?" she asked.

"Not much," he said impatiently. "Will you stick to the point?"

She drew in a deep breath and looked up at him as though this was a hard thing to do.

"Do you know anything about the lost royals of Ambria?" she asked him.

CHAPTER THREE

FOR JUST a second, David thought he'd heard Ayme wrong. Then the implications of what she'd just said crashed in on him. He could hardly breathe.

"Uh, sure," he said, managing not to sound as choked as he felt. "I've heard of them, anyway. What about them?"

She shrugged and sounded apologetic. "Well, Sam claimed Cici's father was one of them."

"Interesting."

He coughed. He'd heard of sightings before. Mostly, they were nothing, led nowhere. But there had been one that had panned out, and when he'd followed up on it, he'd found his oldest brother, the crown prince. There might be more brothers out there. Could it happen again?

"Which one?" he asked, intrigued, emotionally touched, but not really expecting much.

She gazed up at him with those huge brown eyes. "She said he was the second born, and that his name was Darius."

The room seemed to grow and then contract, as though he'd taken a hallucinogenic of some sort. It took all his strength to stay balanced without reaching for support. She was still talking, telling him something more about her sister, but he couldn't concentrate on what she was saying.

Sam had named him...*him*...as the father of her baby. But that was impossible. Incredible. Wrong. Wasn't it?

He did some quick calculations. Where had he been ten to twelve months ago? Whom had he dated? It was true that he'd spent some time over the years finding love in all the wrong places. There had been a period of his younger life when he'd made conquests first and asked questions later—if at all. He wasn't proud of those times and he was sure he'd put them well behind him. But what had he been doing last year? Why was it that he couldn't really remember?

He thought of Cici's cute little face. Was there anything familiar in it? Had he felt a slight connection? Some magic sense of kinship? A tie? Anything?

He agonized for one long moment, searching his heart and soul for evidence. But he quickly decided there was none. No, he was sure there had been nothing like that. It was crazy to even think this way.

"Have you ever heard of him?" she was asking. "Do you know much about him? Any idea where we can even look to find him?"

"We"? He noted the question and realized what it meant. She really did think he was going to drop everything in his life and start helping her, didn't she? The problem was, he would have to do just the opposite. He needed to melt away and very quickly. She didn't realize how dangerous this could be for him. She was sort of like a grenade someone had pulled the pin on and rolled into his apartment. Things could explode at any moment. The smallest jolt could blow everything up.

"No," he said shortly. "What gave you the idea I would know these things, anyway?"

"I told you, I was given your name as someone who might be able to help me."

She was looking nervous. He hated to disappoint her. But this was serious and now it had his complete attention.

"Given my name?"

As the full implications of that began to come into focus, an icy finger made its way down his spine and all his instincts for survival began to stir.

"Who was this who gave you my name?"

"A man associated with my law firm. He deals with Ambrian things all the time and he knew who you were."

He took that in and considered it carefully. But wait. His Ambrian roots weren't known to more than three or four of his closest associates. To most of the world, he was Dutch. How in hell would someone in Texas know otherwise?

"His name?" he said quickly, staring at her intensely, as though he could draw the information out of her if he tried hard enough.

"Carl Heissman. Do you know him?"

Slowly, he shook his head. He'd never heard the name before, at least, not that he could remember.

She shrugged. "I really didn't know him until…"

"How did you get in touch with him? Did you go to him and ask for his help?"

"No, it wasn't like that." She shook her head. "No, not really. I went to the office and asked for a leave and explained about Cici…."

"So how did he contact you?"

"He must have heard about what I was doing from my boss, so he gave me a call."

His heart was thumping in his chest. "He told you my name over the phone?"

"No. Actually, he wanted to meet at a little wine bar downtown. We sat out on the patio."

"Where he couldn't be recorded," he muttered to himself.

"What?" she asked.

She was beginning to wonder why all this was such a big deal to him. Either he could help her or he couldn't. The man in Texas was a side issue as far as she was concerned. She frowned at him, just to let him know she thought he was going off down a blind alley and that wasn't very helpful.

But he wasn't paying any attention to that. He shook his head, his brow furled, obviously thinking things he wasn't sharing with her.

"Go on."

"Well, I thought he knew you from the way he talked. He gave me your name and address and then he even offered to pay for the trip."

David's eyes flared at that bit of information.

"Why would he do that?"

She shrugged. "I thought it was odd at the time, but I assumed it might have been the law firm that was offering to pay. I didn't take anything from him, but…"

"But you don't really know who he is or what his connection to your law firm is, do you? He just came at you out of the blue."

She gave him an exaggerated glare for the interruption, but she plowed ahead.

"I have a number where I'm supposed to call him

when I find Cici's father." She glanced around, looking for a phone. "Do you think I should give him a call?"

He held back the grunt of exasperation he was tempted to mete out. That was obviously the last thing he wanted her to do.

"You haven't called him yet?"

"No."

"Don't."

She blinked. "Why not?"

He hesitated, then shrugged. "You haven't found Cici's father, have you?"

"Maybe not." She eyed him speculatively, her chin high.

He groaned, turning away. He knew he couldn't let her call the number. That would pinpoint his exact location for sure. But how to convince her of that without giving away the entire background?

Whoever this Carl Heissman was, the man was playing games. Deadly games. He had to think fast and get back to basics and consider all possibilities.

He glanced at her again, studied her, tried to pick up on any details he might have missed so far. Why was she really here? Was this a ploy? A plot to coax him out of hiding?

Whatever. He had to get out of here right away and hope whoever was behind sending her here wasn't already on his trail—or worse, here as well and just hadn't revealed himself as yet. He heard a sound behind him and turned quickly, jumpy as a cat.

There was nothing there—this time. That wary buzz was back in full force. Ayme had invaded his space like the point guard of a small enemy army and he was going to have to be on alert every minute. He couldn't afford to trust her or anything about her. His eyes narrowed as he looked her over and considered every angle.

And then the house phone rang.

They stared into each other's eyes for a long moment as it rang once, twice....

Then David took three steps and picked up the receiver, staring down into the identifying screen. Nothing was there. It was blank.

His face turned to stone and his heart beat so hard he could hardly breath. It was never blank. It always said Private Caller if nothing else. But this time, it was blank.

He couldn't answer. That would give the caller absolute knowledge of where he was at this very moment. There wasn't a doubt in his mind that this person wasn't calling in the middle of the night for a friendly chat. This was the danger he'd always known would come his way—and until he understood the exact threat better, it was something he had to avoid at all costs.

And more than that, he had to get out of here.

He turned to look at Ayme, wondering if she'd caught the connotations of this late night call, if she might even know who it was and why he was calling. But her face was open and innocent and her gaze was shining with curiosity. He couldn't believe she could be an expert liar and con artist with eyes like that. No, she didn't know any more than he did. He would have bet anything on that.

"Okay, you've been begging for sleep," he told her, putting the phone back on its cradle. "Why don't you take the spare bedroom around the corner from where you were? Get a few hours sleep. You'll be better for it in the morning."

"Lovely," she said, pure gratitude shining from her eyes for a few seconds. She only hoped that Cici would have as much compassion and give her a chance to get in some real, sustained sleep. Small dozes had been the rule for days.

She glanced at David. His eyes were clouded with some problem he was obviously working through and his handsome face looked a bit tense. That made her all the more grateful.

She was lucky he was taking her presence with such equanimity. Most people would have kicked her out by now, or at least edged her toward the door. But he was ready to let her stay. Thank God. She wasn't sure she could think clearly enough right now to get herself a room in a hotel on her own, especially carrying a baby around. It was great of him to invite her in. She could hardly wait to throw herself on the bed and let sleep take over.

Then she had second thoughts. He hadn't said anything about getting sleep himself, had he?

"What are you going to do?" she asked suspiciously.

He shrugged rather absently, as though his mind were miles away. "I've got some business to wrap up."

She knew it was an excuse, but she didn't push it. She was just too tired to challenge him. The thought of sheets and a real pillow were totally seductive for the moment. So she followed him to the spare bedroom and waited while he carried Cici in, setting her little bed right beside the real bed without waking her at all. He seemed to have the magic touch.

She smiled, watching him tuck Cici in. So precious.

"I'll see you later," he said gruffly, and she nodded,

waiting just until he closed the door before slipping out of her skirt and sweater, leaving only her underclothes on, and sliding between the sheets. She dropped into sleep instantly, but for some reason, she began to dream right away, and her dreams were full of tall, dark-haired men who looked very much like David.

Meanwhile, David was moving fast, preparing to vacate the premises. He'd been planning for this day from the time he could think through the consequences of being found by the vicious Granvilli family who had taken over his country. He knew they wanted all remnants of the Royal House of Ambria wiped out, wherever they might be hiding. They wanted no lingering threats to their ugly reign of terror over the ancient island people.

And he and his older brother Monte were a threat, whether the Granvilli bunch knew it yet or not. At any rate, they were determined to be one. He was already committed to being in Italy by the end of the week to meet with other Ambrians and begin planning in earnest for a return to power. He might as well leave now. There was nothing keeping him here. He'd already made his office aware of the time off he planned to take. He could begin his journey a little early and make his way to Italy in a more careful trajectory. There was no telling what other obstacles he would find along the way.

"Nothing really worth having is easy." Someone had said that once, and right now it made perfect sense to him. The struggle to get his country back was going to be a rough one and he was ready to get started.

And he had to go on his own, he told himself. There was no way to take Ayme along, no reason to do it. Why should he feel this tug of responsibility toward her? He tried to brush it away. She would be okay here. He hadn't even known she existed two hours ago. Why should he feel he owed her anything?

He didn't. But he did owe the people of Ambria everything. Time to begin paying them back.

He had preparations that had to be dealt with, paperwork that had to be destroyed so that the wrong people wouldn't see things they shouldn't see. It took some time to do all that and he had an ear cocked toward the phone in case the interested party from a half hour before might try again. But the night moved relentlessly forward without any more interruptions. The sky was barely beginning to turn pink as he wrapped up his arrangements.

Completely focused, he pulled on a dark blue turtleneck cashmere sweater and finished dressing at warp speed, then glanced around his bedroom. He hesitated for half a second. Did he have time to grab some things and shove them into an overnight bag? What the hell—he had to have something with him, and he'd taken all this time already. Why not? It was all right there and it took no time at all.

He slid into his soft leather jacket as he headed for the door. Despite all the rationalizing he'd been doing, he felt pretty rotten about leaving Ayme behind this way. She was so all alone in the city. She didn't know anyone but him.

That gave him a quick, bitter laugh. She didn't really know him, did she? Which was what was so ridiculous about all this. Still, he hesitated in the open doorway. Maybe he would call the doorman from his car and ask that he look after her. Sure. He could do that. She would be okay.

Right. He took one more step and then stopped, head hanging forward, and uttered an ugly oath. He knew he couldn't leave her.

There was no telling who that had been on the phone There was no telling who was after him—except that he was rock-bottom sure it was an agent for the Granvillis. What if the assassin came into his apartment after he left? Who would protect her? Not the doorman. That was pure fantasy.

No, he couldn't leave her—even if she was the one who had brought all this down on him. He was almost certain that she didn't know anything about it herself. She was an innocent victim. He couldn't leave her behind.

Giving out a suppressed growl of rage, he turned and went back, opening the door to the spare bedroom and looking in.

"Ayme?" he said tersely. "I'm sorry to wake you, but I've got to go and I don't want to leave you here."

"Huh?" She stared up at him, startled, her eyes bleary. She'd had less than an hour of sleep—not nearly enough. "What?"

"Sorry, kiddo," he bit out. "You're going with me." He glanced around the room. "Do you have any other clothes?"

She blinked, trying to get her fuzzy mind to make sense of the question. "I left my bag in the corner." She nodded her head in its general direction.

He stuck out his hand to her. "Come on."

She took his hand in hers and stared at it as though it were a foreign object. "Where are we going?"

He gave her a little tug and she didn't resist, rising halfway out of bed.

"Away from here."

"Why?"

"Why?" He looked into her eyes, alert for any hint of guile. "Because it's too dangerous to stay."

"Oh."

That seemed to convince her. She tumbled out of bed like a sleepy child, pulled the sheet around herself and began to look for where she'd tossed her clothes. He'd started to turn away in order to leave her to it, but something about the picture she made with the fabric twisted around her torso, leaving one shoulder bare and most of both long, golden legs exposed, had him rooted to the spot. There was a fluid, graceful beauty to her that took his breath away and reminded him of something. What was it? Some picture from history, some long forgotten fable…

Ambria. The legend of the lake. It was the familiar story of loss and earned redemption. He could remember sitting in his mother's lap as she turned the pages of the picture book and read the story to him.

"Look, Darius. Isn't she beautiful?"

The lady sat on a large rock overlooking the lake, weeping into her cupped hands, and the flowing garment she wore was very like Ayme's sheet. Funny. He hadn't thought of that scene in years and yet it came back to him so clearly as he watched Ayme leaning over to retrieve her clothes. He'd felt the same tug of compassion as a boy as he felt now.

Well, not the same, exactly. He wasn't a boy anymore and the pang of sympathy was mixed with something else, something that had to do with how creamy her bare skin looked in the lamplight, especially where the sheet pulled low, exposing the soft curve of her breast just beneath a lacy strapless bra.

For some odd reason his heart was beating hard again, and this time it had nothing to do with a phone call.

Ayme looked up and caught the look. She gave him one of her own, but hers was cool and questioning.

"Where did you say we were going?"

"I didn't. Let it be a surprise."

She frowned, not sure she liked where this seemed to be headed. "I don't like surprises." She bit her lip, then tried another idea. "I could just stay here with Cici until you get back."

"I don't know when I'll be back. If ever."

That startled her. "Oh."

"And we don't know who might be coming for a visit. So you'd better come along with me."

"I see." The seriousness in the tone of his voice finally got through to her. "In that case, can you excuse me for a moment?" she asked, politely but firmly pointing out that she needed to drop the sheet and she darn well wasn't going to do it until he was out of the room.

He had the grace to look just a bit sheepish.

"Of course," he said as he began to walk out into the living area.

But then he stopped and looked at her again. What was he thinking? Too much about what she did to his libido and not enough about what she could do to the preservation of his life and limbs.

"Wait a minute," he said, turning on his heel and walking back. "Listen Ayme, I've got to know, and I've got to know right now. Are you wearing a wire or any kind of tracking device?"

That stunned her. She clutched the sheet against her chest. What was this, spy versus spy? In her groggy state of mind, it seemed very bizarre and she couldn't make heads nor tails of it.

"What? What are you talking about?"

"I'm serious. I'm going to have to check."

She backed away, her eyes huge as she realized what he was saying and what it actually meant. She held tightly to her fabric.

"Oh, no you're not."

"Hold on," he said gruffly. "I have to do this. I'm sorry. If you've got anything on you, we've got to get rid of it."

She shook her head firmly. "I swear I don't."

"That's not good enough." He gestured for her to come closer. "Come here."

"No!"

Her voice was strong but it was determination built on sand. She was struck by his demeanor and her will was beginning to crumble around the edges. He wasn't a pervert and he wasn't kidding around. She wasn't sure how she knew this with such certainty, but she did.

"You might be bugged and not even know it," he said earnestly, holding out his hand. "Let me see your mobile."

That she could deliver.

"Be my guest." She tossed it to him, but pulled the sheet even more tightly around her body and was very sure to stay out of his reach, frowning as fiercely as she could muster.

He slid open the little compartment, flipped out the battery and checked behind it. Nothing. He put the battery back and switched it off, then tossed it back to her.

"I'll have to ask you to leave it turned off," he told her. "A working mobile is a basic homing device."

Funny—and sad, but turning off her cell phone would have seemed like turning off her source of oxygen until very recently. But now it didn't really faze her. Most of the people she might expect a call from were gone. The people most important to her no longer existed in her life. With a shudder, she pushed that thought away.

But her mind was finally clearing and she was beginning to realize this whole security exercise was not the normal routine for overnight guests, at least, not in her experience. What the heck was he doing here?

She set the phone down and glared at him. "Would you like to explain just exactly why it's suddenly too dangerous here?" she asked crisply. "And why you feel the need to search for bugs and homing devices? Are you expecting some sort of home invasion? Or just being friendly?"

The corners of his mouth quirked but there was no hint of humor in his blue eyes. "Just being careful," he said evasively. "Crossing all the t's, dotting all the i's. As they say, better safe than sorry."

"Hmm," she said, cocking her head to the side as she gazed at him. "And yet, here I've been feeling safe for all these years without ever once submitting to a strip search. Just foolishly naive, I guess."

Her tone was mocking and he felt the sting. "Ayme, I don't like this any more than you do."

"Really?" Her tone was getting worse and she knew it, but, darn it all, he deserved it. He took a step forward and she took a corresponding step back, staying just out of reach.

"Can you tell me what exactly you're looking for?" she demanded. "Will you know it when you see it?"

"Yes, I'll know it when I see it," he said, nodding. "Now will you just stay put for a minute?"

"I don't think so." She made a sideways move that put even more distance between them.

"Ayme, be reasonable."

"Reasonable!" She laughed out loud. "Reasonable? You call searching me to see if I'm wearing a bug reasonable? I call it unacceptable. And I'm not going to accept it."

"You're going to have to accept it."

"Don't you think any bugs are more likely to be in my clothing or luggage?" she noted quickly.

He nodded his agreement. She was absolutely right. But there was another element to this situation. Now that he'd alerted her to his intentions, he had to follow through without giving her a chance to go behind his back to get rid of anything she might know about that she had on her. He'd started this train down the track and he had to follow it to the end if this was to be in any way effective.

"I'm planning to search your things. But first I need to search you."

He gave her a stern look as he followed her sideways move.

"Hold still."

Reaching out, she quickly dragged a chair between them and gazed defiantly over it.

"Why are you doing this, David? Who's after you? Whom do you suspect?"

He moved the chair aside and stepped closer.

"We don't have time to go into that."

"No, wait," she said, half rolling across the bed and landing on her feet without losing her sheet. Now she'd put the entire bed between them and she was feeling a bit smug about that.

Not that her success would hold up. She knew that. Still, she hoped it was getting through to him that she was not happy about all this and she was not about to give in.

"David, tell me what's changed," she challenged. "Something must have." She frowned at him questioningly. "When you first found me here, you were annoyed, sure, but now it's different. Now you're on guard in an edgier way." Her eyes narrowed. "It was that phone call, wasn't it?"

He hesitated, then nodded. "Yes," he admitted.

"Do you know who it was?"

He shook his head. "No, but it seemed like a wake-up call. It made me realize I was being too casual about you."

"Too casual! I beg to differ."

He stared at her and growled, "Ayme, enough. We need to get going. But first, we've got to check you out. Someone might have put a bug on you somewhere, somehow."

"Without me noticing?"

"That's what they do, Ayme. They're experts at attaching devices to your clothes or your purse or even your body in ways you wouldn't think of."

"Who? Who do you think would do that?"

"I don't know. Maybe this character who gave you my name."

She shook her head, thinking that one over. It didn't make any sense at all. "But he's the one who gave me your address. He already knows where you live. Why would he…?"

"Ayme, I don't know," he said impatiently. "And when you don't know things, it's best to cover all the bases. Will you stand still and let me look you over? I promise I won't…"

"No." Her voice was a little shaky, but adamant. "It won't do any good, anyway. I've seen those TV shows. They have gotten very inventive about hiding things on people. There's no way you can check it all. There's no way I would let you."

He sighed, shaking his head as he looked at her.

"You think I don't know that? I can only do so much, and probably only find something if it's pretty obvious. But I have to try. Look, Ayme, I'm really sorry, but…"

Her face lit up as she thought of a solution. She looked at him speculatively, wondering if he would go for it. With a shrug, she decided she had nothing to lose.

"*I'll* do it," she said firmly, shaking back her hair.

He stared at her. "You'll do it? You'll do what?"

Her smile was bemused. "I'll do it. Myself. Why not? Who knows my body better?" She gave him a grin that was almost mischievous. "You're going to have to trust me."

He stared. Trust her? But that wouldn't work. Would it?

Why not? asked a voice inside his head. *Look at that face. If you can't trust this woman, you can't trust anyone.*

Which was actually what he'd pledged from the

beginning—don't trust anyone. Still, there were times when you just had to make concessions to reality.

"Okay," he said at last. "Go for it. We'll see how you do."

"*I'll* see how I do," she corrected. "You'll be going over my bags and clothes. With your back to me. Got it?"

"Ayme," he began in exasperation, but she signaled that he should turn away. It was pretty apparent that following her orders was going to be the only way to move things along, and they really needed to get going. So, reluctantly, he did as she demanded.

He went through her things methodically. He'd had some training in this sort of search in some security classes he'd taken lately, so he didn't feel as strange handling her panties and bras as he might have under other circumstances. He had to take it on faith that she was doing her part. She chattered away throughout the entire exercise—and he didn't find a thing.

"I really understand, you know," she was saying. "And I want to do a good job at this because I figure, if I'm going with you, the danger is as much to me and Cici as it is to you."

"You got it," he said. "That's the whole point."

"So I just want you to know, I'm really being meticulous."

"Good."

"Searching every place I can think of."

That gave him pictures in his head he didn't want to dwell on and he shook off a delicious little shiver.

"Are you finished?" he asked at last, waiting for the okay to turn around.

"Just about," she said. "Listen, I saw this one show

on TV where they had these little homing signal things sort of stapled into a man's skin. What do you think? Is that really a possibility?"

"Sure."

She hesitated. "Okay then, I've been going over every inch of skin, feeling for any strange lumps, and I haven't found anything suspicious. But just to be safe…"

He turned and looked at her. She was standing just as before with the sheet pulled around her and clutched to her chest, watching him with those huge dark eyes.

"What?"

She sighed and looked sad. "I can't see my back. I can't reach it, either."

He stood very still, looking at her. "Oh."

She licked her lips, then tried to smile. "You're going to have to do it."

"Oh," he said again, and suddenly his mouth was dry and it felt like he hadn't taken a breath for too long.

"Okay, then."

He was willing.

CHAPTER FOUR

THIS was nuts.

David swore softly, trying to get a handle on this crazy reaction he was having. She was just a woman. He'd been with more women than he wanted to think about. He didn't get nervous around females anymore. He'd gotten over that years ago. He'd made successful passes at some international beauties in his day, film stars, rock singers, even a female bull fighter, without a qualm. So why was his heart thumping in his chest as he approached Ayme to check out her back?

She stood there so demurely, holding the sheet tightly to her chest so that it gaped in back, exposing everything down to the tailbone, but not much else. The entire back was there, interrupted only by the slender scrap of lace that was the band of her bra, but that might as well have been invisible. He didn't even notice it. He reached out to push her hair back off her neck, his fingers trailing across her warm skin, and the flesh beneath his hand seemed to glow.

"Okay, I'll do this as fast as I can," he said, then cleared his throat to try to stop the ridiculous quavering he could hear in his voice. "I'm just going to run my hand across your back a few times."

"Get it all," she said, head tilted up bravely. "I can take it." She drew in her breath as his fingers began to move.

"But don't linger," she warned softly.

Don't linger.

For some reason, those words echoed over and over in his head as he worked. Her skin was buttery smooth, summer-day hot, totally tempting, and every inch seemed to resonate to his touch. But he swore to himself that he wasn't going to notice anything, no matter how crazy it made him. He wasn't going to notice how good she smelled or how sweetly her curves seemed to fill his hand.

So why was his breath coming so fast? Why was his body tightening like a vise? This was insane. He was responding to her like he hadn't responded to a woman in ages. And all he was doing was checking for foreign objects on her back.

And being subtly seduced by her gorgeous body. He closed his eyes as he made a last pass down as low as he dared let himself go, and then drew back, saying, "We'd better check your underclothes, too," and heard his voice break in the middle of it.

He swore angrily, feeling his face turn as red as he'd ever felt it turn, but she didn't look back. She reached under the sheet and pulled off her bra and panties in two quick moves and checked them herself.

"They seem clear to me," she said without turning to look at him. "You can check too if you'd like."

"I'll take your word for it," he said gruffly.

This was unbelievable. He felt sixteen again. How had he ended up here? There was a tension in the room that was almost electric. Was he the only one who felt it, or did she feel it, too? It was probably best not to go there. He turned to leave the room without looking at her again.

"Wait," she said. "Do you think I'm clear?"

Reluctantly, he made a half turn back but didn't meet her gaze. "I didn't find any sign of anything, so I guess you are."

"Good. I'm glad. So now you don't suspect me any longer?"

He turned all the way and looked right into her dark eyes. "I suspect everyone, Ayme. Don't take it personally."

She made a small movement meant to be a shrug but almost more of a twitch. "I'm trying not to. But it's not easy."

His gaze was caught in hers and he couldn't seem to pull it away. There had been a quiver in her voice, a thread of emotion he couldn't quite identify, and it had touched him somehow. Looking at her, he felt suddenly confused, not sure how to respond to her.

"Go ahead and get dressed," he said gruffly as soon as he managed to turn away from her. Not looking her way again, he went through the doorway. "We'll get going in just a minute."

She didn't answer and he went into the kitchen, poured himself a glass of cold water and gulped it down, then took in a deep breath and tried to rationalize away what he'd just done.

It wasn't what it seemed, of course. How could it be? He didn't do things like that. His over-the-top reaction to her body was just a symptom of everything else going on around them—the muted fear, the preparations for running, the memories of his own tragic past. Just natural heightened apprehension. Hardly unusual. Nothing to be alarmed about.

She was just a girl.

Relieved and resolute, he went back into his more normal confident action state and returned to the bedroom with a spring in his step. Luckily, she appeared dressed and ready to go and when he looked into her face, there was nothing special there—no regrets, no resentment, no special emotions making him uncomfortable.

"Come on. We've got to get out of here." He slung his overnight bag over his shoulder and reached for the baby. "I'll get Cici. You bring your bags, okay?"

He led the way to the back steps, avoiding the elevator. It was a long, long climb down, but eventually they hit the ground floor, made their way to the parking garage and found his little racy sports car. He made Ayme and the baby wait against a far wall while he prepared for departure.

He'd done everything right. He'd switched out the license plates on the car. He'd checked under the hood and along the undercarriage for explosives. But even so, he winced as he started the engine with the remote, relieved when nothing went "boom."

Another day, another risky move, he thought to himself as he helped Ayme into the car and began packing baby supplies away in all the nooks and crannies. One of these times the click from the starter just might be the last thing he ever heard.

Now the next dilemma—should he head for a big city where they could get lost in the crowd, or for the countryside where no one would ever think to look? For once he chose the country.

But that was still a long way away. First, he headed into a direction directly opposed to where he actually wanted to go. After an hour of driving, he pulled into a protected area and hustled Ayme and Cici out of the car with all their belongings. Then he hailed a cab and they went in a totally different direction, stopping at a garage where he had arranged for another of his cars to be stored. This car was a complete contrast to his usual transportation, small and boxy and not eye-catching at all.

Ayme carefully maintained a pleasant expression. She didn't want to be a whiner. But she couldn't resist, as they squeezed into the small, cramped car, saying "I like the sports car better."

"So do I, believe me," he told her. "This is my incognito car."

"I can see why. You could probably join the Rose Parade unnoticed in this thing."

Glancing sideways, he threw her a quick smile that had actual warmth and humor in it, and she tingled a bit in response. It was nice to know he could do that. She'd been worried that he might be all scowls and furled brows with very little room for fun. But it looked like there was hope. It might not be all sex appeal with him.

She smiled to herself, enjoying her own little joke. She would love to tease him but she didn't quite dare, not yet. If he was right, they were running from danger here. Not a time for light-hearted humor.

Danger. She frowned out the window at the passing buildings. She wished she knew a little more about this "danger" element. Who was this dangerous person and why was he after David?

For just a moment, her mind went back to what had happened in the bedroom just before they left David's apartment. The way her pulse had surged in response to a few hot looks from the man was all the danger she could deal with right now. Clear and present danger. That's what he represented to a girl like she was.

Woman, she corrected herself silently. *You're a woman, darn it. So act like one!*

"You might as well relax," he said, glancing her way again. "It'll be a few hours before we get to our destination."

"I'm relaxed," she claimed. "Don't worry about me."

"Why don't you try to get some sleep while Cici is taking her nap?"

It was a sensible suggestion, but she wasn't in a sensible mood. Despite her bone-aching weariness, she was too full of adrenaline to sleep now.

"But I'll miss the sightseeing," she told him. "I want to see the countryside."

He glanced out at the gaunt, charred-looking buildings they were passing. "We're not going through a lot of countryside right now. More like an industrial wasteland."

She nodded, her eyes big as she peered out at everything, trying to take it all in. "I noticed that."

"Our route is circuitous and it's not going to take us through many of the nicest parts of England I'm afraid. I'm trying to keep it low key and stay away from places where I might see someone I know."

"It's smokestack city so far," she noted wistfully. "Oh, well. Maybe I will try to sleep a little."

"The views will be better in an hour or so," he promised.

"Okay." She snuggled down into the seat, closed her eyes and went out like a light.

He noted that with a sense of relief. As long as she slept, she couldn't ask questions.

He really had mixed feelings about Ayme. Why had he brought her along, anyway? He'd almost left her behind and it probably would have been the reasonable thing to do. But he felt a strange sense of responsibility toward her and of course he wanted to make sure that she was protected.

On the other hand, she probably wasn't going to thank him in the end for dragging her along on this wild-goose chase. She would be better off in a nice hotel in a touristy part of town where she could while away her time shopping or sightseeing or whatever. At the same time, he would have been free to slip in and out of various cities and countries without having to adjust for a baby. After a day hauling a child all over the landscape, she might be ready to accept a solution such as that.

It was a tempting proposition, but there was a major flaw in his thinking and it came to him pretty quickly. Someone out there in the world was fathering babies under his name. This was not helpful to the world situation or even to his own peace of mind. He had to find out who it was and he had to get it stopped. Until he'd managed that, it might be best to keep tabs on the young woman who'd dumped this particular problem in his lap.

Well, that was hardly fair. The problem had been there all the time. He just hadn't been aware of it until she'd arrived on his doorstep carrying the evidence.

But when you came right down to it, all that might be an excuse to keep her around, just because he liked looking at her. He glanced down at her. She was super adorable when she slept.

He had never been one to be bowled over by a pretty face. After all, there were so many pretty faces and he'd had his share of romantic adventures back when he was indulging in that sort of thing. He wasn't going to let a little fatal attraction get in the way of his plans.

He was hardheaded and pragmatic, as he had to be if he and his brother were going to succeed in getting their country back. Romance wouldn't work in times like these, and even a casual flirtation could cloud a man's mind and get in the way of the goal. What he and his brother planned to do was going to be hard, perilous and very possibly fatal.

Relationships were out. Period.

He wondered, and not for the first time, what Monte would think of what he was doing. He wanted to call him but this wasn't the place—nor the time. He had to be somewhere secure. Later—once they found a place near the coast to stay for the night, he would find a way to contact his brother.

She slept for two hours and then woke, stretching like a kitten and looking up at him as though she were surprised to see him.

"Hi," she said. "You're still here."

"Where would I go?" he asked, half amused.

She shrugged. "Since my life became a bad dream, I expect dreamlike things to happen all the time. Maybe a Mad Hatter at the wheel, or at the very least, an angry hedgehog."

"It's a dormouse," he muttered, making way for another car to merge onto the roadway in front of him.

"All right, an angry dormouse." She smiled, amused that he would know the finer points of the Alice in Wonderland story. "So you're neither?"

"Nope. But I have been accused of White Rabbit tendencies in the past." He gave her a sideways grin. "Always late for that important date."

"Ah." She nodded wisely. "Annoying trait, that."

"Yes. They say habitual lateness is a form of selfishness, but I think it's something else entirely."

"Like what?" She was curious since she was always late for everything herself and would like to find a good new excuse for it.

But he never got to the point of telling her. Cici intervened with a long, loud demand for attention from the backseat.

"Wow, she's hungry," Ayme noted, going up on her knees to tend to her over the back of the seat. She pulled a bottle of formula out of the baby bag, regretting that she couldn't warm it. But Cici wasn't picky at the moment. She sucked on the liquid as though someone had been starving her.

"Don't feel like the Lone Ranger, little girl," Ayme cooed at her. "There's a lot of that hunger thing going around."

"Subtle hint," he commented.

"I can get less subtle if it bothers you," she said, flicking a smile his way. "Do we have any food with us at all?"

"Not that I know of."

"Oh." His answer was disappointing, but pretty much what she'd expected. "Are we planning to rectify that anytime soon?" she asked, trying to be diplomatic about it.

He grunted. "I guess we could stop when we see something promising."

"Good. You don't want me to start wailing away like Cici does. It wouldn't be pretty."

She spent the next ten minutes feeding the baby, then pulled her up awkwardly and tried to burp her. David noted the lack of grace in her efforts, but he didn't say anything. She would learn, he figured. Either that, or she would find Cici's father and head back to Texas, free of burdens and swearing off children for all time. It seemed to be one of those either-or deals.

"We need a real car seat for her," he said as Ayme settled her back into the backseat. "If we get stopped by the police, this makeshift bed won't cut it. We'll probably both get carted away for child endangerment."

She plunked herself back into her seat and fastened the seat belt, then tensed, waiting for the inevitable complaints from the back. After a moment she began to relax. To her surprise, Cici wasn't crying. What a relief!

"When I was young," she told David, "my father would put me in a wash basket and strap me to the seat and carry me all over the Texas Panhandle on his daily route."

"Those were the days when you could do things like that." He nodded with regret. "Those days are gone."

"Pity."

He almost smiled thinking of her as a young sprout, peering over the edge of the basket at the world.

"What did he do on his route. Salesman?"

"No, he was a supervisor for the Department of

Agriculture. He checked out crops and stuff. Gave advice." She smiled, remembering.

"It was fun going along with him. My mother worked as a school secretary in those days, so my father was basically babysitting me and my sister." She laughed softly. Memories.

"Sam's basket was strapped right next to mine. As we got older, we got to play with a lot of great farm animals. Those were the best days." She sighed. "I always liked animals more than people, anyway."

"Hey."

"When I was a child, silly. Things have changed now."

The funny thing was he wasn't so sure all that much had changed with her. From the little bit she'd told him of her life, he had a pretty good idea of how hard she worked and how little she played. Someone ought to show her how to have a little fun.

Someone. Not him, of course, but someone.

They stopped at a small general store and he went in, leaving her in the car entertaining the baby. Minutes later he came out with a car seat in tow.

"This ought to do it," he said, and in no time at all they were back on the road, Cici officially ensconced in the proper equipment.

"She seems to like it fine," Ayme noted. "She's already falling back to sleep."

He handed her a couple of sandwiches he'd picked up in the store and she looked at them suspiciously.

"This isn't going to be one of those strange British things, is it?" she asked. "Vegemite or Marmite or whatever?"

He grinned. "Those are Australian and British, respectively. I'm Dutch. We eat kippers!"

"What's a kippers?"

"Kippers are canned herring, usually smoked."

"Fish?" She pulled back the paper. "Oh, no! What is that smell?"

"It's a great smell," he retorted. "A nice, sea-faring nation smell. Lots of protein. Eat up. You'll love it."

She was ravenously hungry, so she did eat up, but she complained the whole time. He ate his own kipper sandwich with relish.

"Good stuff," he remarked as he finished up. For some reason the fact that she was complaining so much about the food had put him in a marvelous mood. "That'll hold us until we get in later tonight."

She rolled her eyes, but more as a way to tease him than for real. Now that she'd had something to eat, she was sleepy again, but that made her feel guilty.

"Would you like me to drive?" she said. "You must be dead on your feet. You need some sleep."

He shook his head. "Do you have a license?" he noted.

"No," she said sadly. "Only for Texas."

"That won't work."

She sighed. "Sorry."

But in another few minutes, she was asleep again.

Just looking at her made him smile. He bit it off and tried to scowl instead. He wasn't going to let her get to him. He wasn't that easy. Was he?

When he couldn't resist glancing at her again he realized that maybe he was. But what the hell, it didn't mean a thing. It was just that she was so open and natural and so completely different from the women he was used to. For years now, he'd been hanging out with a pretty sophisticated crowd. And that was on purpose. He'd found out early that you could find out a lot if you hung with the right people and learned to listen. He had a very large hole in his life. He needed some very specialized information to fill it in.

Twenty-five years before, he'd been woken in the middle of a terrifying night, bundled up and raced out of the burning castle he'd lived in all six years of his young life. He knew now that his parents were being murdered at about the same time. It was likely that many of his brothers and sisters were killed as well. But one old man whose face still haunted his dreams had come to his room and saved his life that night.

Taken by people who were strangers to him from his island nation and smuggled into the Netherlands, he arrived the next day, a shaken and somewhat traumatized refugee, at the noisy, cheerful home of the Dykstra family. He was told this would be his new home, his new family, and that he must never speak of Ambria, never let anyone know anything about his past. The people who brought him there then melted away into the scenery and were never seen again—at least not by him. And there he was, suddenly a Dykstra, suddenly Dutch. And not allowed to ask any questions, ever.

The Dykstras were good to him. His new parents were actually quite affectionate, but there were so many children in the family, it was easy to get lost in the shuffle. Still, everyone had to pitch in and he did learn to take care of the younger ones. He also learned how to listen and quietly glean information. From the very beginning his purpose in life was to find out what had happened to his family and to find a way to connect with any of them who might still be alive. As he got older, he began to meet the right people and gain the trust of the powerful in many areas, and little by little, he began to piece things together.

At first the socializing had just been a natural inclination. But over time he began to realize that these people did move in circles close to the wealthy and the influential, elements that might prove helpful in his quest to find out what had happened to his family—and his country. Over the years various things half-heard or half-understood sent him on wild-goose chases across the continent, but finally, six months ago, he'd hit pay dirt.

He'd been playing a friendly set of tennis with Nico, the son of a French diplomat, when the young man had stopped his serve, and, ball in hand, had stared at him for a long moment.

"You know," he said, shaking his head, "I met someone at a dinner in Paris last week who could be your twin. It was a fancy banquet for the new foreign minister. He looked just like you."

"Who? The foreign minister?"

"No, idiot." Nico laughed. "This fellow I met. I can't remember his name, but I think he was with the British delegation. You don't have a brother in government?"

By now, David's heart was pounding in his chest as though he'd just run a four-minute mile. He knew this might be the break he'd been searching for. But he had to remain cool and pretend this was nothing but light banter. He took a swing into empty air with his racquet and tried to appear nonchalant.

"Not that I know of. All my brothers are happily ensconced in the business world, and spend most of their time in Amsterdam." He grinned across the net. "And none of them look much like me."

He was referring to his foster brothers, but the fact that he wasn't a real Dykstra was not common knowledge and he was happy to keep it that way.

"The ugly duckling of the family, are you?" teased Nico.

"That's me."

Nico served and it was all David could do to pay enough attention to return it in a long drive to the corner. Nico's response went into the net and that gave David a chance for another couple of questions, but Nico really didn't seem to know any more than what he'd said.

Still, it was a start, and the information breathed new life into his hopes and dreams of finding his family. He got to work researching, trying to find a list of the names of everyone who had attended that banquet. Once he had that, he began searching for pictures on the Internet. Finally, he thought he just might have his man.

Mark Stephols was his name. There were a couple of other possibilities, but the more he stared at the pictures of Mark, the more certain he became. Now, how to approach him and find out for sure?

He could find out where Mark was likely to be at certain public events, but he couldn't just walk up and say "Hi. Are you my brother?" And if he actually was, the last thing he could risk was standing side by side with the man, where everyone could immediately note the resemblance between them and begin to ask questions. So as he waited for the right chance, he began to color his hair a bit darker and grow a mustache. There was no point in making identification too easy.

His highly placed social intimates came in handy, and

very soon he obtained an invitation to a reception where Mark Stephols could be approached. Despite the hair dye, despite the mustache, the moment the introduction was made—"Mr. Stephols, may I introduce Mr. David Dyskstra of Dyskstra Shipping?"—their gazes met and the connection was made. There was instant—though silent—acknowledgment between the two of them that they had to be related.

They shook hands and Monte leaned close to whisper, "Meet me in the rose garden."

A few minutes later they came face-to-face without any witnesses and stared at each other as though they each weren't sure they were seeing what they thought they were seeing.

David started to speak and Monte put a finger to his lips. "The walls have ears," he said softly.

David grinned. He was fairly vibrating with excitement. "How about the shrubbery?"

"That's possible, too, of course. Don't trust anything or anyone."

"Let's walk, then."

"Good idea."

They strolled along the edge of a small lake for a few minutes, exchanging pleasantries, until they were far enough from the house and from everyone else, to feel somewhat safe. They looked at one another, then both jockied comments back and forth for another few minutes, neither knowing just what to say, neither wanting to give the game away, just in case what looked true wasn't.

Finally, Monte said out of the blue, "Do you remember the words to the old folk song our mother would sing when putting us to sleep for the night?"

David stopped where he was and concentrated, trying to remember. Did he? What had that been again?

And then he closed his eyes and began to murmur softly, as though channeling from another time, another place. In his head, he heard his mother's voice. From his mouth came the childhood bedtime song in Ambrian. When he finished and opened his eyes again, he turned to his brother. Mark had been still, but tears were coursing down his tanned cheeks. Reaching out, he took David's hand and held it tightly.

"At last," he whispered. "At last."

CHAPTER FIVE

AYME didn't sleep for long, and soon she was up and reacting to the beauty of the countryside.

"I don't know why I haven't come to Europe before," she said. "I've just been so wrapped up in law school and starting a new career and being there for my family."

Her voice faded on the last word and she had to swallow back her feelings. Every now and then it hit her hard. She had to hold it back. There would be a time to deal with sorrow and pain. The time wasn't now.

"And boyfriends?" David was saying. "I'm sure you've got a boyfriend back home."

She settled down, shaking away unhappiness and trying to live in the moment. "Actually, I don't," she admitted.

"Really."

"Really." She thought about it for a moment. She kept meaning to get a boyfriend. So far her life had just been too busy to have time for that sort of thing. "I've been going to college and going to law school and working, as well. There just hasn't been time for boyfriends."

"You're kidding." So it was just as he'd thought. She was a workaholic who needed to learn how to be young while she still had the chance. "Most women make time."

"Well, I didn't. I was so set on doing the very best I possibly could and succeeding and making my parents proud of me."

"Your adoptive parents, right?"

She nodded, biting her lip.

"Ah." He nodded, too. So it was a classic case of over-compensation. She probably spent all her time working frantically to prove it was a good decision for them to have chosen her. "You're the girl driven to bring home the As on her report card."

She smiled fleetingly, pleased he seemed to understand.

"And your sister Sam?"

"Sam not so much." She winced, wishing she hadn't said that. She didn't ever, ever want to say anything that even hinted at criticism of her adoptive sister ever again. She put her hand over her heart, as though she could push back the pain.

"I came over to Texas with a bunch of kids who'd lost their parents in the rebellion. We were all adopted out, mostly to American families with Ambrian roots."

"So it was an organized rescue operation."

"Sort of. I've told you all this, haven't I? I was adopted by the Sommers of Dallas, Texas, and I grew up like any other American kid." Her parents' faces swam into her mind and she felt a lump in her throat. They were such good people. They should have had another twenty or thirty years. It didn't pay to expect life to be fair.

"You don't remember Ambria at all?" he asked after a moment.

She gave him a look. "I was eighteen months old at the time I left."

"A little young to understand the political history of the place," he allowed with a quick, barely formed grin. "So what do you really know about Ambria?"

"Not much." She shrugged. "There were some books around the house." Her face lit up as an old memory came to her. "One time, an uncle stopped in to visit and he told Sam and me about how we were both really Ambrian, deep down, and he told us stories." She half smiled remembering how she and her sister had hung on his every word, thrilled to be a part of something that made them a little different from all their friends.

Ambrian. It sounded cool and sort of exotic, like being Italian or Lithuanian.

"Other than that, not much."

He thought that over for a moment. He'd had the advantage of being six years old, so he remembered a lot. But when you came right down to it, the rest he'd learned on his own, finding books, looking things up on the Internet. His foster parents had taken him in and assumed he was now one of the family and Dutch to boot. No need to delve into things like roots and backgrounds. That just made everyone uneasy. They had been very good to him in every other way, but as far as reminding him of who he was, they probably thought it was safer if he forgot, just like everyone else.

And if it hadn't been for one old man who had moved to Holland from Ambria years before and lived near their summer home, he might have done just that.

"Too bad your parents didn't tell you more," he mused, comparing her experience to his and wondering why such different circumstances still ended up being treated the same way by the principals involved.

"They were busy with their jobs and raising two little girls, getting us to our dance practices and violin lessons and all that sort of thing."

She moved restlessly. This was getting too close to the pain again. She hadn't told him about her parents yet and she wasn't sure she ever would. She knew she would never be able to get through it without breaking down, and she wanted to avoid that at all costs. Better to stick to the past.

"They were great parents," she said, knowing she sounded a little defensive. "They just didn't feel all that close to Ambria themselves, I guess." She brightened. "But being Ambrian got me a grant for law school and even my job once I passed the bar."

He remembered she'd mentioned something about that before but he hadn't really been listening. Now he realized this could be a factor. "Your law firm is Ambrian?"

"Well, a lot of the associates are of Ambrian background. It's not like we sit around speaking Ambrian or anything like that."

This was all very interesting. The Ambrian connection was going to turn out to be more relevant than she knew—he was sure of it. His jaw tightened as he remembered that he still didn't really know why she had shown up in his apartment or who had sent her.

But of course, there was a very possible explanation. She could, even unwittingly, be a stalking horse for a real assassin. Or she could merely be the one testing the territory for someone who meant to come in and make sure David never reached the strength to threaten the current Ambrian regime. It was hard to know and he was more and more convinced that she didn't know anything more than what she'd told him.

He remembered what she'd said about not knowing which side her parents had been on. Since she had no emotional identification with either side, she was pretty much an innocent in all this. If she was here because an enemy of his had sent her, she wasn't likely to be aware of it.

Still, he shouldn't have brought her along. It was a stupid, amateur thing to do. He should probably find a way to park her somewhere—if it wasn't already too late.

Because he couldn't keep her with him. He was due in Italy by the end of the week for the annual meeting of the Ambrian expatriate community. This would be the first time he'd ever attended. It was to be a gathering of the clan, a coming together of a lot of Ambrians who had been powers, or were related to those who had been, in the old days. He needed to be focused on the future of Ambria, not on Ayme and Cici. He couldn't take them along.

So—what to do with them in the meantime?

He'd promised he would help Ayme find Cici's father and he meant to keep that promise. It was bound to get a bit complicated, seeing as how his name had come into the picture, and he didn't have much time. But he had a few contacts. He would do what he could to help.

The only thing he could think of was Marjan, his adoptive sister who was married with two children and lived in a farming town in a northern area of Holland. It was a good, out of the way place where they could melt into the scenery. Maybe even he could slip in below the radar there.

It was odd how quickly he seemed to have slipped into the cloak-and-dagger mold. But then, he supposed he'd been training for it ever since he left Ambria, in attitude if not in action. It was true that he'd never felt he could fully open himself to others in his life. He always had to hide, not only his real identity, but also his feelings about things.

"So I guess you could say," he said, going on with their conversation, "bottom line, that you don't really care about who runs Ambria?"

"Care?" She looked at him blankly. "I've never given it a second thought."

"Of course not."

He turned away, feeling a surge of bitterness in his chest. Was it only he and his brother who still cared? If so, they were going to have a hard time rallying others to their cause. But it was hardly fair to lay this complaint on her. She couldn't help it that no one had bothered to educate her about her background.

And if he were honest with himself, he would have to admit that the strength of his own feelings had been greatly enhanced by his relationship with his brother. Before he knew Monte, his interest in Ambria was strong, even passionate, but diffused. It had taken an intensive experience with his brother to bring out the nuances.

It had been exciting and a fulfillment of a lifelong dream to find Monte the way he did. But it had been very difficult for the two of them to have any sort of relationship. They couldn't trust most forms of communication, they couldn't appear together anywhere because of how much alike they looked, they had to be aware of the possibility that someone was listening every time they spoke to each other. So Monte finally hit upon the perfect scheme—a six-week sailing trip in the South Pacific.

They met in Bali and proceeded from there, getting to know each other and hashing out the possibilities of being royals without a country to call their own. They had huge arguments, even huger reconciliations, they shared ideas, hopes and dreams and emotions, and they ended up as close as any two brothers could be. By the time the six weeks was up, they had both become impassioned with the goal of taking their country back, somehow, someday. To that end, they quickly become co-conspirators and developed a plan.

They decided to continue to go under their aliases. That was necessary for survival. Monte would travel in international circles he already had access to and try to gain information—and eventually supporters—and David would go undercover in the social jet-setting world he knew so well to glean what he could from business contacts on one side and the inebriated rich drones he partied with on the other. Their primary goal was to find their lost brothers and sisters and begin to work toward a restoration of their monarchy.

So he had a very large advantage over Ayme. He certainly couldn't expect her to share his goals when she'd never even heard of most of them and wouldn't know what to do with them if she had.

Their conversation had faded away by now and she spent some time watching the countryside roll past. Morning had come and gone and afternoon was sending long shadows across the land. The countryside was much more interesting now with its checkerboard fields and beautiful green hedgerows and the quaint little towns. This was more like the England she'd expected to see.

But the unanswered questions still haunted this trip as far as she was concerned. Where were they going? And why?

They stopped for petrol and David noticed a park nearby.

"Want to get out and stretch your legs?" he suggested as he maneuvered the car into the little parking lot next to a large tree. "I need to make a phone call."

They got out of the car and he strolled out of listening range. She let him go. There was no reason to resent his wanting privacy, after all.

He looked back as their paths diverged. He didn't want her to get too far away. But he needed to make contact with his brother.

Once he had Monte on the line, he filled him in on Ayme and the fact that he had her in tow. Monte was not enthusiastic.

"You're not bringing her to Italy, are you?"

"No, of course not. I'm taking her to my sister's. Marjan will take good care of her."

"Good."

"But in the meantime, I'd like you to do me a favor."

"Anything. You know that."

"Just information. First I need to know about a car accident outside of Dallas, Texas, sometime last week. A young woman named Samantha Sommers was killed. I'd like a brief rundown of the facts in the case, the survivors, etc."

"I'm jotting down your info as we speak."

"Good. Besides that I'd like anything you can find on Ayme. Her name is Ayme Sommers. She's an attorney for a law firm in Dallas that has a division which specializes in Ambrian immigration issues."

"Will do."

"And here's another one. There seems to be someone—probably in the greater London area—who is fathering babies under the guise of being Prince Darius."

That gave Monte pause. "Hmm. Not good."

"No. Do you think you can make inquiries?"

"I can do more than that. I can start a full-fledged investigation on that one."

"Without identifying your own interest in the case?"

"Exactly. Don't worry. I can do that easily."

"Good. I figure he's either found a way to make time with the ladies using the royalty dodge, or..."

"Or he's an agent trying to flush you out."

"You got it."

"I'm voting for the latter, but we'll see." Monte's voice lightened. "In the meantime, David...a bit of news. I've found the perfect wife for you."

David's head reared back. Despite his overwhelming respect for his brother, that hadn't sat well with him from the beginning.

"I don't need a wife right now," he shot back. "And if I did, I could find my own."

"You can find your own mistresses, Darius," Monte said, his tone containing just a hint of rebuke. "Your wife is a state affair."

David groaned softly, regretting his reaction. Where had his tart response come from, anyway? He and his brother had already discussed this and he knew very well that he needed a wife to help support the cause. The right wife. It was one of the obligations of royalty.

The two of them had pledged that everything they were going to do from now on was going to be for the benefit of Ambria. No self-serving ambitions or appetites would be allowed to get in the way. They were both ready to sacrifice their private lives—and even their actual lives if it came to that. He was firmly committed to achieving their goals. Nothing else mattered.

"Families are the building blocks of empires," Monte was saying blithely. "We need you to be married and to have a solid relationship. We've talked about this before. I thought you were on board."

"I am," David put in hastily. "Sorry, Monte. I'm just a little tired and short tempered right now. Don't pay any attention."

"Good. Wait until you meet her. She's beautiful. She's intelligent. And she's totally devoted to overturning the Granvilli clan's totalitarian regime. She'll fight by your side and rule there, too, when we achieve our goal." He chuckled. "I'm not worried about how you'll react. She'll knock you out when you see her."

"I'm sure she will."

But David grimaced, wondering if Monte wasn't perhaps overselling the case. He'd known a lot of bright, gorgeous and astonishing women in his time. So this was another one of them. Readiness to fight for the cause would be just the icing on the cake. He'd seen it all before.

But he couldn't completely discount Monte's opinion. He'd spent so many years adrift, not knowing where he was going or what he wanted to do with himself. He'd done well in his Dutch father's business, but his heart wasn't in it.

Once he and Monte had found each other, their future trajectory became clear. Now he knew what he was on earth to do. He had a new seriousness and a sense of purpose. His life had meaning after all. Finding the rest of his family and restoring them all to power was all he lived for.

"Keep me apprised as best you can. Let me know where you are if you can."

"I will."

Ringing off, he started back to join Ayme and the baby, stopping only to toss the cell phone into a trash can. You couldn't be too careful and he had a stock of extras, just in case.

The park was pretty and green and centered on a pond with a small bridge over it, creating a lovely vantage point for watching small silver fish swim by below.

"Look, Cici. Look at the fishies," Ayme was saying, holding the baby precariously at the rail and making David laugh. Still, he moved in quickly to avoid disaster.

"She's a little young for a swim," he commented. "Here, I'll take her."

And he did so easily. Ayme sighed. It seemed to come naturally to him and she was having such a hard time with it.

She watched him for a moment. He glanced up and caught her eye, but she looked away quickly, still uneasy, still not sure what the point of all this was. The questions just kept bubbling up inside her and she needed some answers.

"Okay, here's what I don't understand," she challenged him as they walked through the grass. "If you're Dutch, how come you care so much about Ambria? What is your tie to the place?"

He looked startled, then like a man trying to cover something up. "Who says I care so much about Ambria?"

"Oh, please! It resonates in everything you say."

Hmm. That wasn't good news. He was going to have to be a bit more guarded, wasn't he? Still, it did seem churlish to keep such basic information from her. It would all be common knowledge soon enough. Once he got to Italy, all would very likely be revealed anyway. He decided she deserved to be among the first to know. Just not quite yet.

"We can talk about this later," he said evasively.

"Wait a minute," she said, stopping in front of him and putting her hands on her hips. "I'm staging a small rebellion here."

Her dark eyes were flashing and her pretty face was set firmly. He knew better than to laugh at her, but it was tempting. She did look damn cute.

"What are you talking about?" he asked instead.

She sighed, shaking her head. "I don't get it. What the heck are we running from?"

"Danger."

"What danger? From whom?" She threw her hands up. "I don't see what I've done to put myself in danger. All I did was hop on a plane and come to England looking for Cici's father. How did that put me in danger?"

He raked fingers through his hair and looked uncomfortable. "It hasn't exactly. It's put *me* in danger." He took in a deep breath and let it out again, slowly. "And because you're currently attached to me, it's put you in danger, too."

Her chin rose and she watched him with a hint of defiance in her gaze. "Then maybe I should unattach myself."

She was just throwing that out there, waiting to see what his reaction would be. When you came right down to it, the thought of "unattaching" from him filled her with dread. At this point, she didn't have a clue what she would do without him. And she really didn't want to find out.

"Maybe you should," he said calmly, as though it didn't mean a thing to him. "It's a good idea, really. Why don't you do that? We can find you a nice hotel and get you a room...."

She observed the way he was holding the baby, so casual, so adept, and she looked at his handsome face, so attractive, so appealing. Did she really want to trade this in, danger and all, for the sterile walls of a hotel room on her own? Wouldn't she just end up trudging from place to place, trying to find someone who could help her?

Hmm. Good luck with that.

Maybe she ought to reconsider before this went too far. She wasn't going to detach herself from him until she had to. Who was she kidding, anyway? She was going to stick around and see what happened. She knew it. He probably knew it, too.

"On the other hand," she said in a more conciliatory tone, as they began to walk again, "if you would just let me know what's going on so I could understand and be prepared, it would be nice. I'd like to be able to make plans for myself once in a while." She searched his face hopefully. "It would be a big help."

His jaw tightened. "You want to know what's going on."

"Yes, I do."

He nodded. She was really a good sport. She deserved more information than he'd been giving her. He couldn't tell her everything. But he could do a better job than he'd been doing so far. He shifted the baby from one arm to the other, stood in one spot with his legs evenly spaced, like a fighter, and looked into her eyes. He was taking a risk in telling her. But what the hell—life was a risk. And despite everything, his gut feeling was that he could trust her.

"Okay Ayme, here's the deal. I am Ambrian. You guessed right from the beginning."

"I knew it!" Her eyes flared with happy sparks and she wanted to grab him around the neck and give him a triumphant kiss, but she restrained herself admirably.

"There's more."

He glanced at her, his intensity burning a hole in her skin and as she realized how seriously he was taking this, her victorious satisfaction faded.

"I've been working with other Ambrians determined to overthrow the usurpers and get our country back."

She gaped at him, suddenly feeling as though her bearings had been yanked away.

"No kidding," she said softly, feeling shaky. "No wonder there are people after you."

No wonder. That was a choice he'd made. But she hadn't made that choice, so what the heck was she doing putting herself and the baby in this sort of jeopardy?

Maybe she was going to have to tell him thanks, but no thanks, after all. Time to say goodbye?

His face was hard and serious and his tone was low and intense as he went on.

"The people who run Ambria right now have spies everywhere. They are very much interested in trying to destroy any opposition they see beginning to crop up. That's why I have to be careful and why I'm afraid of being tracked."

"Okay." She folded her arms across her chest and hugged herself worriedly. "Now I get it. Thank you for telling me that." She blinked up at him, her eyes wide, a picture of pure innocence. "Believe me, I won't betray your confidence."

He wanted to kiss her. Looking down, the urge swept over him. Her face was so fresh and honest, her lips full and slightly parted, her cheeks red from the outdoor air and he didn't think he'd ever seen anyone look prettier. The urge passed. He didn't act on it.

But it left behind another feeling—guilt.

She trusted him.

Ah, hell, he thought.

Guilt filled his throat. He was still lying to her, still leaving things out. She didn't know he was actually the man she was seeking. Well, that wasn't exactly the case, but close. If she knew who he really was, she would be able to focus better on finding the real father. On the other hand, maybe she would just believe he had fathered the child himself. Then what?

There would be no time for DNA tests. He had to be in Italy in less than a week. And he couldn't tell her about that—not yet. Probably not ever. After all, she wasn't going with him, so why did she have to know?

They went back to the car and packed everything away, including the now-sleeping baby, then climbed in themselves and started off. But all the while, he was thinking about their conversation.

There was still so much he couldn't tell her, but he could tell her a bit more than he had.

"Here's some more truth, Ayme," he told her after a few miles. "The truth is, I'm just like you."

"Like me?"

"Yes. I'm an Ambrian orphan, too. I was adopted by a Dutch family right after the rebellion. Just like you."

She thought about that for a moment. It seemed to fit the scheme of things nicely and it gave her a warm feeling of bonding with the man. Though when she glanced at his face, she didn't see any reciprocating on the bonding thing. He appeared as much as ever as though his profile had been hewn in stone.

So now she had some important information and she could use it to fill in the blanks. She knew why David was afraid someone was after him. And she knew why he felt such deep feelings for Ambria. And she knew why he might have connections in the Ambrian community that would help her find Cici's father. But she didn't know...

Turning to face him again, she confronted him with a steady gaze.

"Okay, mister," she said firmly. "Let's have it. More truth. I understand why you might have felt you had to take off from your apartment. And why you want to keep on the move. But what I don't understand is this—why did you bring me along?"

CHAPTER SIX

THAT was a very good question and David wasn't sure he had the guts to answer it, even to himself. He looked at Ayme.

He'd meant a quick glance, but something in her pretty face held him for a beat too long and he had to straighten the car into the proper lane when he put his attention back on the road.

That was a warning—don't do that again.

For some reason Ayme's allure seemed to catch him up every time. He didn't know why. She was pretty enough, sure, but it was something else, something in the basic man-woman dynamic that got to him, and he didn't seem to be able to turn it off.

"Come on, David," she was saying. "Tell me. Why did you bring me along?"

He shrugged and tried to look blasé. "Why do you think?"

She made a face. "My charm and beauty?" She managed to put a sarcastic spin on her tone that made him grin.

"Of course."

She rolled her eyes. "No, really. What was the deciding factor?"

He glanced at her, then looked back at the road and put both hands firmly at the top of the wheel.

"Okay, if you want me to be honest about this, I'll tell you." He hesitated and grimaced again. Since this seemed to be the time for truth why not go a little further? She could handle it.

"This won't be easy for you to understand. You'll think I'm overstating things. You might even think I'm a little nuts. But just hear me out and then decide."

"Of course."

"There are a couple of things going on here. First…" He took a deep breath and went on. "I've always had good reason to expect that someone would try to get to me and kill me someday and I'm not going to talk about why."

She sat very still, but she made a small grating noise, as though she were choking. He ignored it.

"When you arrived on my doorstep I had to consider the possibility that you, or someone who sent you, might be involved in something like that."

"David." Her voice was rough. "You thought I could be a killer?" The idea shocked her to her core.

He looked her full in the face and shrugged. "You bet. Why not?"

She sputtered and he went on.

"But it's more likely to be your Carl Heissman person. Don't you see that? And if I have you with me, you can't contact him and let him know where I am."

She made a gasping sound. "David, what have I done that would lead you to think—"

"Not a thing. And believe me, Ayme, I don't suspect you of anything at all. It's the people who sent you who have me on guard."

"Sent me?" She shook her head, at a loss. "Nobody sent me. I came on my own."

"Someone found out your plans, sought you out and gave you my name. Why?"

She stared at him, realizing he had a point. She remembered that she had been surprised when Carl Heissman contacted her and wanted to meet. He'd been friendly, concerned, charming and her doubts had quickly evaporated. But now that David brought them up again, she had to acknowledge them.

She could see that but, still, this all seemed crazy to her. People killing people was something she just wasn't used to. Assassinations. Killers. Spies. Those things were on TV and in movies, not in real life.

Was he for real or just some insane paranoid? But the more she studied his beautiful face, the more she was sure he believed every word he said.

Did that make it all true? Who knew?

"There's one little problem with that whole scenario," she pointed out right away. "If you left me behind, I wouldn't have known where you were within minutes of your leaving. So how could I tell anyone anything?"

His mouth twisted sardonically. This was obviously not a new thought to him. But all he said was, "True."

She waited a moment, but he didn't elaborate and she frowned.

"Anyway, I thought you were just protecting me from the bad guys, whoever they may be. Isn't that what you said?"

"I did say that, didn't I."

She frowned again, watching him as though she was beginning to have her doubts. "But we don't know who the bad guys are. Do we? I mean, we know they're these

Ambrian rebel types, but we don't know what they look like or what their names are. Right?"

"You're absolutely right. Rather a dilemma, don't you think?"

"Kind of nuts, that's what I think." She shook her head. "Maybe we should have stayed in the apartment. Maybe if we just stayed in one place and waited for them to show up, we'd find out who they are."

"We'd find out more than that. Not a good idea."

"Maybe. But you can't live your whole life just running all the time. Can you?"

"I don't know. I've only just begun."

She made a sound of exasperation and he grinned.

"We have a destination, Ayme. We're not just running for the fun of it."

"Oh. How about letting me in on where that destination is so I can share that feeling of comfort?"

"Not yet."

Her sigh had a touch of impatience to it. "In that case, I'm just useless baggage. So I still don't see why you brought me along."

"Because I feel some responsibility toward you. You came and you asked me for help. Isn't that enough?"

"So you're really planning to help me?" she asked as though surprised that such a thing might be the case.

"Of course. I told you I would."

She settled back and tried to think. What was the old expression, jumping from the frying pan into the fire? That was pretty much what she felt like. She'd been feeling vulnerable enough just searching for Cici's father. Now she was still searching for the man and being tracked by assassins, as well. And everyone knew what happened to people who hung out with people who were being tracked by assassins. Nothing good.

It was like reaching the next level in a video game. Suddenly the danger was ratcheted up a notch and you had to run that much harder.

From what she could gather going over the information he'd relayed, he was part of a revolt against the current regime in Ambria. Too bad she didn't know more about it so that she could decide if he was a good guy or not. From his point of view, he was obviously the "goodest" of the good guys, but that sort of thing tended to be a biased assessment. A strange thought came to her unbidden. What if he considered her a hostage?

The beginnings of a wail from the backseat interrupted her musings and gave notice that Cici was awake again.

"Uh-oh, here we go," Ayme said with apprehension.

David gave her a look. "You seem to live in dread of this baby waking up. She's barely announced her presence. And actually she's been quite good all day."

She sighed. She knew she shouldn't be taking it out on the baby. Still. "You don't know what it was like on that airplane crossing," she told him.

"Babies on planes." He nodded, thinking it over. "Yes, I have to admit that is not a pleasant prospect. But it was probably the pressurized cabin. It probably hurt her little ears."

"You think so?" That put Cici in the category of someone transgressed against instead of the transgressor. She looked back at the baby and gave her a thumbs-up.

"Sure," he said. "It's not likely she's going to cry that way all the time."

He was right. She hadn't been all that fussy lately. But Ayme attributed it to David's calming influence. It certainly had very little to do with her. She only wished she knew the secrets of how to reassure a baby and get it to stop howling.

Cici was awake but gurgling happily as they came into the seaside area where they were going to spend the night.

"Where are we going to stay?" Ayme asked, looking longingly at the Ritz as they cruised past it. Then there was the Grand with its long, sweeping driveway and uniformed attendants standing ready to help guests as they arrived at the huge glass doors. They zipped right by that one, too.

"It's just a little farther," he said, leaning forward to read a street sign.

She noticed that the farther they went from those elegant hotels, the farther they also went from the bright lights and sparkling entryways. Soon they were surrounded by gloom.

"Here we are," he said at last, pulling into a driveway that immediately plunged them down a dark tunnel and into a broken-down parking lot. "This is the Gremmerton."

She took note of the oily puddles and stained walls. "Might as well be the Grimmer-ton," she muttered softly to herself.

"What was that?" he asked, glancing at her as he parked and shut off the engine.

"Nothing," she said, feeling sulky and knowing she was being a brat. "Nothing at all."

He grimaced. He knew exactly what she was thinking but he didn't bother to explain why they were staying here. She would have to figure it out for herself. When you were trying to travel below the radar, you had to stay in places where people would never expect to find you. And at the same time, you had to be low key, so that people wouldn't look at you and sense the incongruity and say among themselves, "Hmm. What is someone like that doing here? You would think someone like that would be over at the Grand."

"We're running low on formula," he noted as they unloaded the car and prepared to carry things up into the room.

"I saw a small market on the corner when we drove up," she said. "If you'll watch her for a while, I'll run out and get some. After we get settled in."

"Good."

They climbed two flights of stairs and found their room. It wasn't really too bad, although it did have wallpaper peeling from one corner and a single light bulb hanging down from the ceiling.

It also had only one bed.

She stared at it for a long moment, then turned to look at him, perplexed. "What are we going to do?" she asked. "Maybe we can order in a rollaway."

"No," he said calmly. It was fascinating watching the sequence of emotions as they played across her face. "We're pretending to be a family. We'll share the bed."

Her eyes widened. "I don't know if we ought to do that," she said, gazing at him with huge eyes.

That one statement, along with her horrified look, told him everything he needed to know about the state of her innocence—as well as the state of her media-fed imagination. He bit back a grin and coughed a bit before he could respond.

"Ayme, do you think I'm not going to be able to control myself? Do you really think I'm going to attack you during the night?"

She looked very stern. Evidently that was exactly what she was worried about.

"Okay," she said. "Here's the honest truth. I've never slept in a bed with a man."

"No!" He pretended to be surprised, then wished he hadn't. He didn't want her to think he was mocking her. It was really very cute that she was so concerned. Compared to most of the women he'd become accustomed to, it was delightful.

"No, really," she was saying earnestly. "I don't know what will happen. I...I don't know men very well." She shook her head, eyes troubled. "You read things..."

"Ayme, don't pay any attention to what you read."

He reached for her. It seemed a natural enough instinct to comfort her. He took her pretty face between his hands and smiled down at her.

"Pay attention to what I tell you. I won't pretend I'm not attracted to you. I am. Any man would be. But it doesn't mean a thing. And anyway, I can handle it. I'm not going to go mad with lust in the middle of the night."

She nodded, but she still seemed doubtful. What he didn't realize was that she was reacting to only one of the things he'd mentioned: the fact that to him being attracted to her didn't mean a thing.

He'd realized by now that he shouldn't have touched her at all and he drew back and shoved his hands into the pockets of his jeans. Then he frowned, watching emotions play over her face and wishing he'd never started down this road.

But now she could add missing the wonderful feel of his warm hands on her face to the fact that to him, she didn't mean a thing. He'd actually said that. Any attraction between them was a biological urge, nothing more. She could have been any woman, it would have been the same.

Wow, she thought sadly. *Talk about crushing a girl's spirits. Didn't mean a thing.*

But what did she expect? She looked at him, at how large and beautiful he was. He was an exceptional man. He probably dated a lot of exceptional women. And he probably thought she was young and silly. Meanwhile, she'd begun to think that he was pretty wonderful.

He cleared his throat, wishing he understood women. She appeared unhappy and he didn't know if it was because of the bed situation or if something else was bothering her. "So let's just play this by ear, okay?" he tried hopefully.

"Okay," she said softly.

"You sleep on your side, I'll sleep on mine. If it would make you feel better, we can make a barrier down the middle with pillows."

Her smile was bright but wavering. "Like an old Puritan bundling board?" she said.

"If you want."

She seemed to be somewhat reassured, but he wasn't. He could still feel the softness of her face against his hands. He shouldn't have touched her.

"Where's the bathroom?" she asked, looking about the room.

"Down the hall," he said. "You can't miss it."

"What?" Ayme shuddered. This on top of everything. "Down the hall?"

"That's right."

"Oh, no, I can't share a public bathroom." She was shaking her head as though this were the last straw. "Are you crazy?"

"This is the way old hotels are set up," he told her. "You'll have to get used to it. You'll be okay."

"I won't," she cried dramatically, flopping down to sit on the edge of the bed. "Bring me a chamber pot. I'm not leaving the room."

She bit her lip. Deep inside, she was cringing. That hadn't really been her, had it? Couldn't be. She didn't play the drama queen, didn't believe in it. But it seemed a combination of circumstances had come against her all at once and for just a moment, she'd cracked.

She was tired, she was scared, she was exhausted, and she didn't know where she was going or what was going to happen once she got there. It was no wonder she was on edge.

But she didn't have to take it out on David. When you came right down to it, he was being very patient. In fact, he was a super guy. Which made it that much worse that she was having a silly tantrum. She could feel her cheeks redden.

Slowly she raised her gaze to his.

"Okay," she said. "I'm done."

"You sure?"

She nodded.

"I'm sorry," she said, trying not to cry. "I'll go check out that powder room now. I'm sure it will be lovely."

It took all his strength to keep from laughing at her

sweet, funny face. He pulled her to her feet by taking both hands in his.

"Come on. You can do it. Others have and lived to tell the tale."

He smiled down at her as she looked up. He was so close. For a fleeting second or two, she had a fantasy, just the flash of an image, of what it might be like if he would kiss her.

But that was ridiculous. There was no reason for him to kiss her. This was not a kissing situation, and anyway, they weren't in a kissing relationship. And never would be. Besides, any feeling between them didn't mean a thing. Hadn't he said so?

Get it out of your head, she scolded herself silently.

Sure, there had been a couple of hot looks between them when they had struggled over the body search incident. And certainly, his hands on her skin had sent her into some sort of sensual orbit for a moment or two. But that was just natural sexual attraction stuff. It might have happened with anyone.

Maybe.

She had to face facts here. She knew her own nature and was inclined to try to find a little romance in almost anything that happened. When she saw a film or a TV show and there was no love interest, her attention would wander. She wasn't a deep thinker. Speculative theories could hold her interest for just so long and no longer. What she wanted to see and to think about was people loving each other.

Maybe it was because she'd never had a real romance of her own. She kept hoping, but no one really wonderful had ever come her way.

Until David, a little voice inside was saying.

Well, she couldn't deny he was pretty darn good. Still, he could never be for her and she knew it. Right now they were thrown together. They were hiding. They were running from someone. They were both taking care of a baby. There wasn't much romantic in all that, but it did keep them involved. She was just going to have to learn to keep his theory in mind at all times.

No matter what happened, it didn't mean a thing.

And then, gritting her teeth, she made her way down the hall and found that the bathroom wasn't nearly as bad as she'd expected. In fact, it was rather cozy, with newer decorations and more accessories than the hotel room itself.

The worst thing was the huge mirror set over a vanity area with a chair and small table. There she was in living color, looking even more horrible and haggard than she'd thought. She was a mess. Her hair resembled a bird's nest. Her eyes were tired and the dark circles beneath them were epic. She groaned and immediately went to work, splashing water on her face and pinching her cheeks to get some color in them. As she tried to comb her hair into a more pleasing tangle, she realized what she was doing and why she was working so frantically to make herself look a bit better. She cared what David thought of her.

"Doggone-it," she whispered, staring into her own eyes in the mirror. There was no hope. He'd already seen the worst of her.

She made her way to the corner market and found a brand of formula that looked like it would do. She was standing in line at the cashier when it occurred to her that she didn't have the right money.

"Uh-oh." She made a pathetic face to the bored-looking young woman behind the counter. "All I have are American dollars. I don't suppose..."

The cashier shook her head, making all her many piercings jangle at the same time. "Nah. We've had some bad experiences. We don't accept American money after six."

Ayme stared at her wondering what difference the time made. "Uh...what if I...?"

"Sorry," the girl said dismissively, pursing her brightly painted lips and looking toward the customer behind her.

Ayme sighed, starting to turn away. She might as well go back, climb the two flights of stairs, get some proper money from David, and do this all over again. But before she could vacate the premises, someone else had intervened, stepping forward to stop the clerk from going on to the next customer.

"Allow me, madam," he said with a gracious nod of his head. In his hand was exact change. He gave it to the clerk with a flourish.

Ayme gasped.

"Oh. Oh, thank you so much." She smiled at him, thoroughly relieved. What a nice man. He looked like her idea of what a composer or conductor should look like—eyes brightly seeing something over the horizon, white hair flying about his head, seeming to explode out from under a smallish felt hat, a supernatural smile as though he could hear music from the heavens. All in all, she thought he looked delightful, and she was so grateful she was bubbling with it.

"You are so kind. This is incredible. I wouldn't accept it but I'm just so tired tonight and the baby is out. But

I do have the money. If you'd like to come with me to the hotel room where we're staying..."

Even as she said the words she realized this wasn't a good idea. They were supposed to be in hiding, not inviting in strangers. She made a quick amendment to her suggestion.

"Please, give me your name and address so I can make sure you get repaid."

He waved all her protestations away. "Don't think twice about it, my dear. It's not a problem." He tipped his hat to her and turned to go. "I hope you have a safe journey to the continent."

"Thank you so much."

She smiled, but as he disappeared into the crowd on the street, her smile faded. How did he know she was on her way to the continent? She barely knew that herself. But this seaside town was a bit of a launching location for trips across the channel. So maybe she was taking his words too seriously.

Still, it did give her pause.

"I assume we're going to the continent?" she said as she returned to the room and began to unpack the little bottles of formula. David already had Cici sound asleep in her new car seat, tilted back and rigged as a bed. "Is that our next move?"

"Yes. Tomorrow we'll be crossing the channel," he told her. He gave her a quick glance to make sure she was suffering no lasting damage from the earlier trip into a public facility, and the fact that she looked calm and pleasant seemed to confirm that all was okay.

"Heading for France?" she asked hopefully.

France! Paris! She would love to see it all.

But he gave her an enigmatic smile and avoided the issue.

"Possibly," he said.

"Or possibly not," she said mockingly, making a face.

He grinned.

"I almost didn't get the formula," she told him as she began to set up a feeding for Cici. She explained about the cashier and the white-haired man.

"It was so nice of him," she said.

Alarms went off in David's head but he quickly calmed himself. After all, she was a very attractive woman. Any man worth his salt would have stepped forward to help her in a moment of need. He would have done it himself. Hopefully that was all there was to it.

Still, he was wary.

"What did he say?" he quizzed her. "Tell me every detail."

"Oh, he was just a nice old man," she insisted, but she told him everything she could remember, and he couldn't really find anything extraordinary in it.

"Let me know if you see him again," he told her. He briefly considered changing hotels, but then he decided he was being a bit paranoid. There was really no reason to suspect the man of anything at all. "Right now I want you to lie down on that bed."

"What?" she said, startled.

His mouth twisted. She was so predictable on certain subjects.

"I want you to get some sleep. I'm going out for a while, but when I get back, I'll take care of Cici should she waken. We may have to take off at an odd hour. I want you to take this chance to get the rest you need."

She turned to look at him. He was handsome as ever, but his eyes did look tired.

"But what about you? You're the one who's been driving and you need some sleep yourself."

He gave her his long, slow smile that he only handed out on special occasions. "I never sleep."

She laughed, charmed by that roguish smile. "Oh, please. What are you, a Superhero?"

"Not quite. But close."

It occurred to her that she knew precisely what he was—wary and mistrustful of something. What exactly did he think was going to threaten them? What was it he was running from? He'd given her a brief sketch of his theories, but not many specifics. She wished he would tell her so she could worry, too.

"Ayme, do what I say," he said firmly when she still hadn't moved. "We don't have time for long, drawn-out discussions."

"Aye aye, sir," she said, sitting on the edge of the bed.

"That's the spirit," he said approvingly. "Consider this a quasi-military operation. I'm the superior officer. You do what I say without questioning anything."

She rolled her eyes dramatically. "Oh, that'll be the day!"

"Indeed." He shook his head and turned to go. "I have to go out to make a phone call."

"Why can't you do it from here? Don't you have your cell phone?"

"I've got my mobile," he responded. "But it's not the phone I want to use for this call."

"Oh." More likely, she thought, it was a call he didn't want her to overhear.

"I'll be back."

She didn't bother to ask again. It was confusing at times. For whole moments he would seem to warm to her, and that special connection would spark between them. Then, in an instant, it was gone again. She wished she knew how to extend it.

But she had other things to think about. She got up off the bed and puttered for a bit, putting clothes away in the closet and cleaning off the dresser of things David had thrown there. Cici still slept. Maybe she would be able to get that nap in as David had suggested she do.

Something drew her to the side window, and peering down into the gathering gloom, she could see the walkway along the front of the hotel. Suddenly, she caught sight of David. He had a cell phone to his ear and seemed to be carrying on an energetic conversation with someone. She could see him gesticulating with his free hand. As she watched, he ducked into the side alleyway beside the hotel and she lost sight of him. She wondered who he was talking to. Hopefully it was someone who knew Cici's father.

Funny how she always thought of him that way— Cici's father—instead of Darius, the Ambrian Prince, or the lost royal. Was that because, deep down, she was pretty sure that either Sam had been fooling her or someone had fooled Sam. The story didn't really seem to hold together. But maybe David would find out the truth.

It was interesting how she trusted him and she really didn't want to analyze why that was. She had a feeling it had something to do with a deep need for a sense of stability in her life. She wanted him to be good. Therefore, he had to be good. Simple as that.

She looked at Cici. Babies were so adorable when

they slept. She was starting to get a handle on how to care for a baby. At least, she thought she was. She was trying to copy everything that David did. It was obvious that a strong, steady hand, a soothing tone of voice and a sense of confidence made all the difference. Cici hadn't been crying much at all and that was certainly a relief.

"I'm a fast learner," she muttered to herself. "I will survive."

Turning from the window, she lay down on the bed and fell instantly to sleep.

CHAPTER SEVEN

DAVID had made a couple of calls, but now he was talking to his brother again. Monte had some information on the requests he'd made earlier. Ayme's background checked out perfectly. She did have an adoptive sister named Sam who had a few teenage arrests for petty crimes and who had died in a car accident just days ago. But that wasn't all. The girls' parents had died in the same accident.

"That's odd," David said almost to himself, reacting to the horror of what Ayme must have gone through. "I wonder why she would have held that back from me?"

"Never trust a woman, David. You aren't falling for her, are you?"

"Hell, no. Give me some credit, okay?"

"Sure, I'm only kidding. I have no doubt about your ability to hang tough. But on to other matters, there is nothing new on the impostor pretending to spread your love about the land. I'll let you know as soon as I hear anything."

"Thanks."

"In the meantime, there's news. Our Uncle Thaddeus has died."

"Oh, no." David felt real remorse. He was the last of

the old guard. "That's a shame. I was looking forward to meeting him someday, and hopefully hearing stories about our parents and the old days."

"Yes, so was I. It is not to be. But his funeral is another matter. We must go to it."

David frowned "Are you serious?"

"Yes. As luck would have it, the ceremony will be held in Piasa during the clan reunion gathering. It will be a huge affair. He's considered the patriarch of the Ambrian expat community. Everyone who means anything to Ambria will be there. It's our chance to begin to step forward and take the reins of the restoration movement. Whoever takes charge at the right time is going to rule the future." He paused, letting the importance sink in.

"Darius, you must come. I need you by my side."

"Of course. If you need me, I'll be there."

Monte gave him the details. "The town will turn Ambrian for a few days, it seems."

"Our covers will be blown."

"Yes."

David smiled. "Thank God."

"Yes."

They both laughed.

"Don't forget. Italy. Be there or be square."

"You got it."

He rang off, bemused and filled with conflicting emotions. He was looking forward to Italy. It was bound to be an exciting, important lesson about his own past, as well as a chance to lay the foundations for a new future. But as he turned back toward the hotel, it was Ayme and the information he'd heard about her parents that filled his thoughts.

He went back up to the room and opened the door quietly. Ayme and Cici were both sound asleep. There was only one light on in the room, in the far corner, and he left things that way, pulling off his sweater and unbuttoning his shirt but leaving it and his jeans on as he came to the bed he was going to share with Ayme.

Looking down, his gaze skimmed over her pretty face, her lovely bare shoulder, the outline of her leg beneath the sheet. She appealed to him, no doubt about it. He waited as the surge of desire swept through him. That he expected. But what surprised him was another feeling that came along with it, a tightening in his chest, a warmth, an unfamiliar urgency. It took a moment to understand what it was, and when it came to him, he closed his eyes and swore softly.

Everything in him wanted to protect her. Every instinct wanted to make sure no one could hurt her.

Where had that come from? He didn't think he'd ever felt that before. He'd spent so much of his life protecting himself, he hadn't had the capacity to worry about others. In other words, he was a selfish, self-centered jerk. And he could accept that. So where had this new soft-headed urge to nurture come from?

Maybe it was just because of the baby. Maybe he was blurring the lines between them in a visceral way he couldn't control. He knew he needed to watch that. It could put him in unnecessary trouble. He didn't want to go doing anything stupid.

More likely the facts that he'd just learned about Ayme's parents' fate had something to do with it. And maybe it was just that he was so damn tired. Could be. He knew he needed sleep. And there was a bed right in front of him. Too bad it was already occupied.

She'd been so shocked by the thought of them sleeping together this way, he sort of hated to spring it on her with no warning, no time for her to prepare. But he wasn't a predator. He was just a sleepy guy right now. And the bed was just too tempting to pass up. With a sigh, he began to prepare for getting some sleep.

Giving a half turn, Ayme gasped.

There was a man in her bed!

Luckily, it was David. This was just what she'd been afraid of. Could she really allow this? Didn't she have to make a stand or something?

But maybe not. He still had his jeans on, but his chest was bare. Still, he was fast asleep and completely nonthreatening. She relaxed and went up on one elbow to look at him in a way she hadn't been able to do before.

She'd been telling the truth when she'd said she'd never had a serious boyfriend. She'd done some dating in college, but it never seemed to come to much. Most men she'd met had either disappointed or annoyed her in some way. The type of man she attracted never turned out to be the sort of man she thought she wanted in her life.

So far David hadn't annoyed her. But he wasn't trying to hit on her, either. Her mouth quirked as she realized that if his disinterest went on too long, that in itself might get to be annoying.

"You're never satisfied," she accused herself, laughing at the paradox. "Picky, picky, picky."

No doubt about it, he was about the most handsome man she'd ever been this close to. She liked the way his lustrous coffee-colored hair fell over his forehead in a sophisticated wave that could only have come from a high-end salon. Then she laughed at herself for even thinking that way. This was no time to dilute her Dallas roots.

"Hey," she whispered to herself. "He's got a good haircut."

But the rest of him was purely natural and didn't depend on any artifice at all. His features were clear and even, his brows smooth, his nose Roman, his chin hard and newly covered with a coat of stubble that only enhanced his manliness. He looked strong and tough, but he also looked like a good guy.

And then there was the rest of him. He had a build to make any woman's heart beat a little faster—something between a Greek statue and an Olympic swimmer. His skin was smooth and golden and the tiny hairs that ran down from his beautiful navel gleamed in the lamplight. His jeans were the expensive kind and his shirt was crisp and smooth, despite all it had been through in the day. His hands were beautiful, strong but gentle. She leaned a little closer, taking in his clean, male scent and the heat that rose from his body, feeling a sudden yearning she didn't really understand. It was tempting to lean down and touch her lips to his skin. She leaned a little closer, fantasizing about doing just that, about touching that belly button with her tongue, about running her hand along those gorgeous muscles.

Then she looked back up into his face and found his blue eyes wide open and staring right at her.

"Oh!" she gasped, ready to jump back away from him, but his hand shot out and stopped her.

"Don't make any sudden moves," he whispered. "Cici is stirring."

She stayed right where she was, just inches from his face.

"So," he said softly, his eyes brimming with laughter. "I guess I caught you checking me out."

She gasped again and turned bright red on the spot.

"I was doing no such thing," she whispered rather loudly, her eyes huge with outrage.

"Oh, yes, you were." He was almost grinning now. "I saw you."

"No, I was just..." Her voice faded. She couldn't think of anything good to pretend she'd been doing.

"Hey, it's only human to be interested," he said softly, still teasing her. "Come on, admit it. You were interested."

"I'm not admitting anything," she whispered back. "You're not all that wonderful, you know. I mean, you may be tempting, but I can resist you."

Somehow that didn't come out quite the way she'd meant it and she was blushing again. His iron grip on her wrist meant she was trapped staying close. So close, in fact, that she could feel his breath on her cheek. It felt lovely and exciting and her mouth was dry. The laughter in his eyes was gone. Instead something new smoldered in his gaze, something that scared her just a bit. She couldn't stay here against him like this. She pulled back harder and this time he let her go.

She swung her legs off the bed and sat up, looking back at him. "I...I think I'll get up for now," she said. "I think you should get some sleep and...and..."

He pulled up and leaned on one elbow, watching her. "I think sleep is going to be hard to find for a while," he said dryly as Cici began to whimper. "We might as well both get up."

She rose and went to the baby and by the time she'd pulled her up and turned back, he was up and putting on his sweater.

"I'll go down and get some food," he said. "I'm sure you're hungry by now. Fish and chips okay for you?"

"More fish?" She wrinkled her nose.

"It's good for you." He hesitated. "I could probably find an American hamburger somewhere, if that's what you want."

"No, actually I like fish and chips just fine. As long as the fish isn't kippers."

He grinned. "Don't worry. They don't make them that way too often."

He left the room and she sighed, feeling a delicious sort of tension leave with him. He'd said it didn't mean a thing, but she was beginning to think he'd been fooling himself. For her, it was meaning more and more all the time.

The fish and chips were okay and so was the pint of ale he brought back with them. But now it was time to tend to Cici and hope to convince her to go back to sleep so that they could get some rest, as well. After a half hour of pacing back and forth with a baby softly sobbing against her shoulder, Ayme had a proclamation to make.

"I've decided I'm not going to have any children," she said with a flourish.

"Oh." David looked up from the evening paper he'd picked up with the fish. "Well, it might be best to hold off until you get married."

She glared at him. "I'm not going to do that, either."

He smiled. "Right."

"I'm serious about this," she insisted. "Babies take over your life. It's unbelievable how much work they are."

"It's true." He had some sympathy for her state of mind. He'd been there himself. "They do monopolize all your time. But that doesn't last forever."

"It certainly seems to last forever on the day you're doing it."

He leaned back. "That's just for the moment. Before you know it, they're heading out the door with their friends and don't need you at all anymore."

She gave him a long-suffering look. "How long do you have to wait for that lovely day?"

"It takes a while."

"I'd be marking off the days on my calendar."

He grinned. "It can be hard, but think of the rewards."

"What rewards?"

Cici stirred in her arms, stretching and making a kitten sound. He watched as Ayme's fierce look melted.

"You see?" he said softly.

She smiled up at him ruefully. "Yeah, but is it all really worth it?"

He shook his head. How the hell had he become the family practices guru here? Still, she seemed to need some sort of reassurance and he supposed he could do that at least.

"Once you have one of your own," he told her, "I think you'll figure that out for yourself."

He rose and took Cici from her, and as he did, he thought of what Monte had told him. He'd thought from the beginning that there was a sense of sorrow lingering in her gaze, something deeper than she was admitting to. Why hadn't she told him about her parents? She must have a reason. Or maybe, as Monte hinted, it was a sign that he shouldn't trust her.

But what the heck—he didn't trust anybody, did he?

"Ayme, you've said you don't know much about your birth parents and you don't know much about Ambria. What exactly do you know?"

She scrunched up her nose as she thought about it. "Just a few things I've picked up casually over the years."

"You should know more."

She looked at him and made a face. "How much do you know?"

"I don't know as much as I should, either. I should have learned more."

"So we're both babes in the woods, so to speak."

He nodded, though there was obviously a vast gulf between what he knew and what she did. "Why weren't you more curious?"

She didn't answer that one, but she had something else on her mind.

"You were adopted just like I was," she noted. "Didn't you ever feel like you had to...I don't know. To prove to your parents that they should be glad to have picked you?"

He stared at her. "Never," he said.

She shrugged. "Well, I did. I was always trying so hard to make them proud of me."

He could see that. He could picture her as a little girl in her starched dresses with patent leather mary janes on her little feet.

Cici had finally fallen asleep and he laid her down in her little car seat bed before he turned toward Ayme again.

"And were they?" he asked softly, his gaze taking in every detail of her pretty face. "Proud of you, I mean."

"Oh, yes. I was the perfect child. I made straight As and won awards and swam on the swim team and got scholarships. I...I think I did everything I possibly could." A picture swam into her head. She'd entered the school district Scholars' Challenge, even though she was the youngest competitor and she was sure she had no chance. Jerry, a boy that she liked, had tried out and hadn't made it. He mocked her, teased her, made her miserable for days, saying she'd only made it on a fluke, that she was going to be the laughing stock of the school.

By the time the night of the competition rolled around, she didn't like him much anymore, but he had succeeded in destroying her confidence. She went on stage shaking, her knees knocking together, and at first, she didn't think she could hear the questions. She panicked. Jerry was right. She wasn't good enough. She looked to the side of the stage, ready to make a run for it.

Then she looked out into the crowd. There was her mother, looking so sweet, and her father, holding a sign that said Ayme Rocks. They were clapping and laughing and throwing kisses her way. They believed in her. There was a lump in her throat, but she turned and suddenly she knew the answer to the question, even though she thought she hadn't heard it right. She was awarded ten points. She wasn't going to run after all. A feeling of great calm came over her. She would do this for her parents.

She won the trophy for her school. Her parents were on either side of her as they came up the walk at home. Suddenly, her mother stepped ahead. She threw open the doors to the house, and there inside were friends and neighbors tooting horns and throwing confetti—a surprise celebration of her win. It was only later that she realized the celebration had been planned before her parents knew she would win. They were going to celebrate her anyway.

Thinking of that night now, tears rose and filled her eyes and she bit her lip, forcing them back.

"I think I made them very happy. Didn't I?"

Her eyes were brimming as she looked up into his face as though trying to find affirmation in his eyes.

He couldn't answer that for her, but he took her hands in his and held them while he looked down at her and wished he knew what to say to help her find comfort.

She took in a shuddering breath, then said forcefully, holding his hands very tightly, "Yes. I know I did." She closed her eyes, made a small hiccupping sound and started to cry.

He pulled her into his arms, holding her, rocking her, murmuring sweet comforting things that didn't really have any meaning. She calmed herself quickly and began to pull back away from him as though she were embarrassed. He let her go reluctantly. She felt very good in his arms.

"Sorry," she murmured, half smiling through her

tears. "I don't know what made me fall apart like that. It's not like me to do that."

"You're tired," he said, and she nodded.

He waited, giving her time, wondering when she was going to tell him her parents had died in the accident, but she calmed down and began to talk about a dog she had found when she was young.

"And what about Sam?" he asked at last, to get her back on track.

Now that she had unburdened herself this far, he felt as though she might as well get as much out in the open as she could bear. A catharsis of sorts.

And she seemed to want to talk right now. There was a little couch in the room and they sat down side by side and she went on.

"See, that's the flip side of it," she said. "The dark side, I guess. The better I did, the worse Sam seemed to do." She tried to smile but her face didn't seem to be working right at the moment. "The more I seemed to shine, the more Sam rejected that path. She became the rebel, the one who didn't succeed, on purpose. She got tattoos against our father's orders and got her nose pierced and ran around with losers."

"That sounds pretty typical. I've seen it before."

"I guess so." She shrugged. "Funny, but I can see it so much more clearly now than I ever did then. I knew she resented me." She looked up quickly and managed half a smile. "Don't get me wrong. We shared a lot of good times, too. But the undercurrent was always resentment. I used to think if she would just try a little harder… But of course, she felt like I'd already taken all the love slots in the family. There was no room for her to be a success. I'd already filled that role. She had to find something else to be."

"That must have been hard on your parents."

"Oh, yes. But in some ways, they didn't help matters. They weren't shy about telling Sam what they thought of her."

"And comparing her to you?"

"Yes, unfortunately. Which didn't help our relationship as you can imagine."

"Of course."

"So Sam left home as soon as she could. By the time she showed up with Cici, she'd been mostly gone for years, off with some boyfriend or another and only coming back when she needed something. She broke our parents hearts time and time again. And then, suddenly, there she was with a baby in her arms. Of course, part of us was thrilled. A new member of the family. But at the same time, my parents were horrified. Where was Cici's father? Had there been a wedding? I'm sure you can guess the answer to that one."

"I think I can."

"She was penitent at first. I think she'd been under a lot of stress trying to deal with a baby on her own. But once she got some good sleep and some good food, she quickly became defiant again. And when Mom tried to get her to make some realistic plans she had a tantrum."

"That was helpful."

"Yes. It was later that night that she told me who Cici's father was. She came to my room to ask me to take care of Cici. She claimed she'd tried motherhood and it didn't agree with her. So she was taking off."

"Just like that."

"Just like that."

"What did you say?"

She turned to him. "What do you think I said? I got hysterical." She threw up her hands. "I couldn't take her baby. I...I refused and I yelled a lot. I told her either our parents would have to raise her...or we'd have to put her up for adoption."

"Ouch."

"Oh, yes. I said horrible things." She looked at the sleeping baby. Was she looking at the situation any differently now? "Things I didn't mean. But I was trying to get her to face reality. She had the responsibility. She couldn't just shrug it off."

"And yet, somehow that is the way it worked out."

She nodded.

"She took the keys to my mother's car and drove off into the rainy night."

"And your parents went after her?"

"Yes. And they found her quickly enough."

"And?"

She flashed him a stiff smile. "There was an accident. And Cici became my problem."

He watched her, puzzled. Why not take that next step and tell him her parents had died in that accident, too? What was holding her back? It was a horrible thing and she was probably still reeling from the shock of it. But surely it would be better to open up about it, work through it, put it in some sort of context with her life. Until she did that, he was afraid she would have that look of tragedy deep in her eyes. And what he wanted most for her—wanted with a deep, aching need—was happiness.

CHAPTER EIGHT

Cici was fussy during the night and Ayme and David took turns walking her. That way, they both got enough sleep and in the morning they were actually feeling rather refreshed and ready to face another day.

And it was a beautiful morning. They ate a quick breakfast and then went walking along the stone path that led to the marina, watching the morning sun glint over the silver sea and the breeze shuffle some puffy white clouds across a cerulean sky. Cici was good as gold, her big blue eyes wide as she looked out at the world, so new and fresh in her young gaze.

Ayme had found a little stash of cute clothes in the bag, things she hadn't packed and didn't remember, so she'd been able to dress the baby very stylishly for their morning walk.

"This is the fun part, putting them in cute clothes," she told David.

"I never knew that," he said doubtfully. "Somehow that never appealed to me."

"Live and learn," she advised him with a sassy smile.

He grinned. He liked her sassy smile. In fact, he was beginning to realize he liked a lot about this young woman. Too much, in fact. But he wasn't going to think about that this morning. He was going to enjoy the weather, the scenery—and her.

They watched ships and boats sail in and out of the harbor, watched the fishermen come in with a catch. They listened to the sounds, smelled the sea odors and breathed in the sea air. Then it was time to go back and they walked slowly toward the hotel. David felt a strange contentment he wasn't used to. Cici made a cute, gurgling sound and they both laughed at her. He smiled. What a cute kid.

But whose kid?

Was there really a chance that he could be Cici's father? He'd racked his brain trying to remember who he'd been dating almost a year ago. He was afraid it was rather emblematic of his lifestyle that he was having so much trouble. What did it prove? Maybe nothing. But it did mean he'd had encounters with women that meant nothing to him, didn't it? And that wasn't anything to be proud of.

He was virtually certain he couldn't be the baby's father. And yet, one tiny little doubt kept nagging at him. It was the kind of thing where you woke up in the middle of the night and stared at the ceiling as the thought whirled in your brain, larger than life. During the day, it faded into irrelevancy, hardly noticeable. And yet, it wouldn't fade completely away and leave him totally alone.

He was thinking about it when Ayme suddenly whirled and pointed toward a man disappearing around a building.

"Look! There's the man from the little store last night."

He turned and looked but the man had disappeared. "What man?"

"The white hair…didn't you see him?"

"No. Who is he?"

"I don't really know, but he was very sweet to me last night at the convenience store. Remember? I didn't have enough money and he paid for me. Actually, I owe him some money. Keep a look out, maybe we can flag him down and I can pay him back."

The entire incident put David on alert. In his current frame of mind, seeing anyone twice on their itinerary was seeing them too often. He swore softly.

"Damn," he said as reality flooded back. "We're going to have to go."

"Go?" She turned to look at him. "Go where? Why?"

There was no point in trying to explain to her. She would just ask more questions. Besides, they didn't have the time.

"Come on, hurry. We've got to get going."

"Okay, but tell me why."

"I wanted to wait until dark," he said instead. "Everything's easier in the dark."

"Or harder, as the case may be."

"True." He flashed her a quick grin. "Let's pack up and get out of here post haste."

Ayme was hurrying along, but rebellion was smoldering in her heart.

"David," she said softly. "Tell me what we plan to do."

"Get away from your white-haired man."

"What? Why? He was very nice."

"Most assassins are great guys to go bowling with,"

he told her from the side of his mouth. "You can look it up. It's in the statistics."

She looked at him and shook her head. He wasn't taking her request seriously and it was beginning to make her angry. Swinging around in front of him, she blocked his path into the hotel and confronted him, hands on her hips.

"You know what? You need to give me a reason for all this. I can't do things without a reason. I'm a methodical, logical thinker and I really need to know why I'm doing things."

He seemed annoyed but tried to be patient. "I will. I promise you. Just give me a little more time."

She threw up her hands. "For all I know, we could be on our way to rob a bank or knock over a candy store or kidnap a famous hockey star or...who knows?"

"None of the above," he assured her, though he knew she was just using those as examples. "Ayme, we don't have time for this. We'll talk once we're on the road."

She sighed. She knew she wasn't going to be able to stand her ground. Not yet. But if he kept this up...

"Oh, all right," she said, and they raced for the stairway.

They were able to get a slot on the service that packed cars in for the trip through the tunnel, and they made it in record time. A short time later, they were back on the highway, on the French side of the channel.

Ayme was excited. After all, this was part sightseeing trip for her. But when David made a left turn where she was expecting a right one, she protested.

"Hey, the sign says 'Paris, that way'."

He glanced at her warily. "But we're not going to Paris."

Her heart sank. "Where are we going?"

"You'll see."

She bit her tongue. She'd had just about enough of this "you'll see" stuff. If he didn't trust her enough to let her know their destination at this point, what was she doing with him?

And then she had a brief moment of self-awareness and she realized she really ought to stop and think about what she was doing, period. Why was she running around the countryside with this man she barely knew? It was bad enough that she'd dropped everything to race to London with Cici on a mere address and a whim. But what was she doing now? This was crazy. His apprehension of being in danger was obviously sincere or he wouldn't be taking these measures to stay hidden. And here she was going right along with him—as though she were meant to. Insanity!

But she knew very well why she was doing it. Of course, his being such a gorgeous hunk of male humanity didn't hurt. There was a spark between them; she wouldn't deny that.

But there was something more, something deeper, something worse. She was doing it to avoid reality.

Funny, that—she'd jumped headlong into a dangerous chase in order to avoid her real-world situation. It seemed a contradiction. But she knew it was pretty accurate. Anything beat sitting around and thinking about her life. The longer she stayed on this journey to nowhere, the longer she could put off dealing with what had happened to her sister and to her parents. And the longer she could put off facing what the rest of her life was going to be like.

Okay, so she knew why she was doing this. And she

knew why he was doing this—at least she had a good idea. But that didn't mean she had to sign on to this "you'll see" business any longer. Either she was a partner in crime, or she would bail out of this situation. Well, maybe not bail exactly. But she would let him know she wasn't happy and insist on better treatment.

She settled back and looked at him, at his beautiful profile and his sexy day's growth of dark beard, at the way his gorgeous, shiny hair fell over his forehead. He glanced her way and frowned.

"What?" he said. "What's the matter?"

She didn't answer. She just kept looking at him. He glanced her way a few more times, and finally, with an exclamation of exasperation, he pulled over to the side of the road and turned to face her.

"What's wrong?" he demanded crankily. "You're driving me crazy with this silent routine. Tell me what you want."

She stared hard into his starry blue eyes. "Trust," she said at last. "I want to be trusted."

From the puzzled look on his face, she could see he had no idea what she was talking about.

"I trust you," he protested.

"No, you don't. If you trusted me, you'd tell me the truth."

A wary look suddenly clouded his gaze.

"Ah-ha!" she thought. There was evidence of guilt if she'd ever seen it.

"The truth about what?" he asked carefully.

"Everything," she said firmly.

Everything. He let his head fall back against the headrest and chuckled softly. If she only knew how much more complicated that would make it all.

"Ayme, Ayme, what makes you think I actually know the truth about anything?"

"You know more than I do. And that's all I want." She moved closer, touching his arm with her hand, trying to make him understand just how important this was to her. "You see, this is what I hate—you knowing and me not knowing. You guiding and me following without a clue. I need to be in control of my own destiny. I can't just sit here and let you control my fate. I have to have some free choice in the matter." Her fingers tightened on his arm. "Give me facts, let me make my own decisions. Let me make my own mistakes. But don't treat me like a child, David. Please. Let me be your partner."

He looked into her earnest face and felt a wave of emotion different from anything he'd ever felt before. He liked her. He liked her a lot. Too much, in fact. But he didn't care. There was something so good and true and valuable in her. Reaching out, he cupped her cheek with the palm of his hand and smiled into her eyes. The urge to kiss her bubbled up in his chest. Another urge competed. He wanted her to have whatever she wanted in life and he wanted her to have it right now. He wanted to protect her and be there for her and, at the same time, to let her fly free.

But mostly, he wanted to kiss her. He was moving closer, looking at her pretty lips. He could already taste her….

But wait. Swearing softly, he pulled himself up short. Someone had to. Taking a deep breath, he slipped his hand from her face and looked away and pulled himself together. What the hell was he doing here?

Frowning fiercely, he got tough.

"You want some facts, Ayme? Okay, here you go. I've

had word that there definitely are people following me. It's not all in my mind after all."

An early morning call to Monte had given him that information.

"I think your white-haired man may be one of them."

"Oh."

"Right now I'm trying to think of a way to get us to a safe place I know of without the bad guys knowing for sure where we are. So we are headed for a nice Dutch farm area to the north. My sister lives there. If we make it there without something bad happening, we're going to stay with her for a bit."

She sighed. That was all she wanted, a little sign that he trusted her, at least a little.

"Thank you," she said earnestly. Then she smiled. "That sounds nice. I always like people's sisters."

He watched her face light up and he groaned inside. The temptation to kiss her was with him all the time now. Every time he looked at her, he could feel what her body would be like against his and all his male instincts came to life. He had to find a way to ratchet his libido down. The whole sexual attraction thing was a new way to complicate his life and he had to resist it.

"I'm sure she'll like you, too," he said gruffly.

She nodded happily. "Okay then. Lead on."

And he did.

But he knew very well that the information he'd given her would only be the beginning. It was human nature. Once you had a taste, you wanted more. They hadn't driven for half an hour before she was asking questions again.

"So who exactly are these people who are following you?"

He shrugged. "I assume they are agents of the regime in Ambria. But I don't know that for sure."

"Because they know you are working against them?"

He nodded. This was no time to get into the rest of the reason.

She frowned thoughtfully, biting her lip. "We need something to call them. The Bad Guys is too generic."

"You think?"

"Yes, I do." She thought for another minute or two. "I've got it. Let's call them the Lurkers."

He shrugged, amused by her urge to organize everything. "Sounds fair."

She smiled, obviously pleased with her choice.

And she was pleased with Holland, too.

"It's so beautiful here," she said after a few hours of watching the landscape roll by. "It's like a fairy tale. Everything is so cute and clean."

"That's the Netherlands," he agreed. "It's quite a nice place."

"And you grew up here."

"That I did."

"Did that make you into a nice person?"

He grinned at her. "It's good to see you've noticed," he told her.

She smiled back at him. That spark thing happened and they both looked away quickly. But Ayme was warmed to her toes and floating on a cloud.

By late afternoon, they had arrived at the outskirts of the town of Twee Beren where David's sister lived.

"Here's another news flash for you, Ayme," he said

as he began to navigate the tiny streets. "If my current plan works out, we'll be making our way to my sister's house in a farmer's hay wagon. How's that for local color?"

"Oh. That's interesting." Though she was a bit taken aback at the prospect.

"I thought you'd like that. Hope Cici can take all the straw."

"The straw?" Ayme blinked at him. "What straw?"

"We'll be in hay. Straw." He gave her a puzzled glance. "You do know what a hay wagon is, don't you?"

"I...I think so. In fact, I think I've been on one before when I was a little girl and going around to the different ranches with my father."

"There you go. You should be an old hand at this."

"Hmm."

"The thing is, I'm sure the people following us...."

"The Lurkers, you mean."

He nodded, his wide mouth twisted in a half grin. "The Lurkers. They have the license number on this car, so we have to ditch it somewhere unobtrusive in the town. Then we'll switch over to the hay wagon. That ought to throw them off."

"I know it does that to me," she muttered, shaking her head, wondering what on earth he was thinking.

He pulled into a parking space near a vacant lot, switched off the engine, and turned to her. "Okay, here we go. We have about two blocks to walk. I'll carry Cici. Try to look inconspicuous."

She gazed at him, wide-eyed. "How do I do that?"

He looked her over. She was right. She was gorgeous with the afternoon sun shining in her golden hair.

Everyone within a half mile would be craning their neck to see her.

"Think ugly," he said, knowing it was no use. "Here, wear this wool cap."

She put it on and now she resembled a ragtime street urchin. He smiled. He couldn't help it. She was so darn adorable.

But someone else walking by was smiling at the picture she made, too, and he frowned.

"Come on. We're becoming a spectacle just trying not to be one. It's no use. We'll have to hurry along and hope we blend in."

They gathered their things, packed in a sleeping Cici and made their way down the street and around the corner to where a rather mangy-looking horse stood hitched to a relatively flat farmer's wagon. Hay was piled on it high as a hay stack and it had been left right in front of a small, friendly seeming pub.

David nodded with satisfaction.

"Good. Some things never change. Old farmer Shoenhoeven has been stopping here for his afternoon drink for as long as I can remember. When he leaves for home, he goes right past my sister's farm." He grinned at his own memories. "It's been fifteen years since I last did this. And to think the old man is still going strong. How old must he be? He seemed ancient back when I was a kid."

"You know him? Do you think he'll give us a ride?"

"He'll give us a ride but he's not going to know about it," David said, scanning the street. There weren't many people out and about. "We can't sit up there with him for all to see. We're going to hide in the back of his wagon."

"We're going to do what?" She came to a screeching halt and whirled to face him, appalled. "Even in Texas we don't do stuff as goofy as that."

"Well, here in Holland, we do." He looked around the quiet street again. There was no one in sight.

"Come on. As you walk past, turn in a little. There's a place where you can climb up. See the foothold? Just swing yourself up and make a dive under the straw."

She turned to face him, horrified. "Are you kidding me?"

"Hurry, Ayme," he commanded in a tone that brooked no debate. "Before someone comes around the corner."

"But…"

"Now!"

She threw her hands into the air but she did as he said. He came right behind her, handing off the baby and pushing back the straw so that they would all fit beneath it. They scrunched in, lay side by side under the straw and stayed very still. Ayme was holding her breath, listening intently, but no one came along to challenge their right to jump aboard.

"Is Cici okay?" David asked in a low voice at last.

Ayme looked at the baby, then blew a small piece of straw out of her mouth before she answered. "She's still asleep. Can you believe it?"

Carefully, she laid the baby down on a blanket between two wooden boxes, making sure no straw was touching her face. Then she turned back to David. They'd made a little cave in the straw and it was actually rather cozy. The corners of her mouth quirked.

"This is really silly," she whispered to him. "I feel like my feet are sticking out the bottom. Like the witch in *The Wizard of Oz*."

He grinned at her, leaning on his elbow and looking incredibly handsome with his eyes dancing and hay in his hair.

"Do I look like a farm boy?" he asked her, chewing on the end of a long straw.

"Uh-huh."

"Hush," he told her. "Or we'll have people calling in to the police about checking out a talking hay stack."

She couldn't meet his gaze without giggling. "Here we are in the back of a hay wagon." She was laughing out loud. Then she hiccuped and laughed harder.

"Shh," he hushed warningly, reaching to quiet her.

"This is just so funny, it's so ridiculous," she said between hiccups. "I mean, what are we doing here?" She was laughing again.

"You're getting hysterical," he warned near her ear.

"I'm not hysterical. You're tickling me."

"I'm not tickling you."

"Your breath. It tickles my skin."

Somehow that very concept sent her into new gales of laughter that she tried to stifle, but couldn't. He was on the verge of laughing, too, just from watching her. But she had to be quiet and stop making the haystack move if they were going to get away with this. And she showed no inclination to do so.

So he kissed her. As far as he could see it was the only option, short of throttling her.

It was meant to be a quick shock to her system, a way to stop the laughter in its tracks. A warning. A suggestion. A way to keep her from harming them all. But it turned into much more than that.

When his mouth covered hers, her lips parted immediately and her tongue flickered out as though to coax him inside. He took that invitation and made his move and then everything began to blur. His senses went into red-velvet mode. Everything about her felt soft and plush and everything he touched seemed to melt before him. He'd never felt anything this wonderful before. He never wanted to stop.

And neither did she. Every other man she'd ever kissed had been a wary exercise in testing waters that she hadn't found very warm, nor very tempting. This was so different. She felt as though she'd reached for a ripe fruit and had fallen over a cliff just as she grabbed it. It was a fall that had her spiraling from one level of delicious sensation to the next. She never wanted to reach the bottom of that canyon. She wanted to fall forever, as long as she was in David's arms.

She stretched. She reached for him—she was begging for more. His embrace was such a comfort to her, such a warm, safe place to be. She sank into the kiss as though she'd finally found a place where she really belonged.

But not for long. He pulled back, cursing himself silently for being such an idiot. This was exactly what he'd been warning himself against. He couldn't do this. It was stupid, but most of all it wasn't fair to her.

"I'm sorry," he said, hair falling over his eyes as he looked down at her. "I didn't mean to do that."

"Shh," she said, eyes wide. "He's coming."

They listened, quiet as mice, while the man called out his goodbyes and started to sing as he came toward the wagon.

Ayme gasped. "David, he's drunk!"

"Nah."

"Yes, he is," she whispered near his ear. "Listen to him."

"He's not drunk-drunk. Just a little tipsy. He's had his evening Bols and he's floating a bit. That's all."

The farmer climbed up into the driver's seat and called the horse to attention, and they started off. The wagon creaked loudly. The horses hooves clanged against the pavement. And the farmer sang at the top of his lungs.

"He's definitely had too much to drink!" Ayme hissed at David.

"Yes," he admitted. "Yes, he has. But it's okay. This isn't like a car. The horse knows the way. He'll take over."

"The horse!" She shook her head at the concept.

"You can always count on the horse. Out here in the country, you can fall asleep at the wheel…or the reins, I guess it is…and the horse will still get you there."

She wasn't sure she bought that one. "How do you know all this?"

"I used to live out here. Every summer, we spent at least a month in the country."

The wooden wheels hit a rock and they all bounced into the air.

"Ouch. This is bumpier than I remember. I guess my bones are older now."

Ayme was laughing again, which made him laugh. She was right. This whole thing was crazy. But at least they might be losing the Lurkers, leaving them in the dust. He certainly hoped so. He didn't know for sure what they wanted, but he knew he didn't want to give it to them. And he had a feeling it probably had something to do with an effort to keep him from showing up in Italy at the end of the week. That only made sense.

He was glad he'd thought of going to Marjan's. She was the closest to him in age of all his adoptive siblings. They'd been quite close growing up. She was married now and living a mile or so outside the little village of Twee Beren. He hadn't been able to call ahead, but he knew she would be happy to see him. She always was. Hopefully, she would be happy to take in Ayme and Cici until he could find Cici's father. That would leave him free to maneuver, and free to meet Monte in Italy. And that would get him away from the temptation Ayme was beginning to represent. The sooner the better for that.

They didn't have to be as sneaky bailing out as they had been climbing in. The farmer was singing so loudly, he wouldn't have noticed a brass band piling out from under the straw.

And then the farmhouse was right before them. David rang the bell and a pleasant-looking, slightly plump woman answered, took one look at them and threw her arms around her brother's neck without a word.

Ayme watched, just a step away, and then she followed them into the large, comfortable house while Marjan explained that her family was away and she was alone.

"Hans takes the children to see his mother every year for her birthday, and usually I go, too. But this time I had promised to make pies for the cheese festival in town, so here I am, rolling out pie dough all day instead."

David was glad he only had one person to try to explain things to. He'd been wondering just what he was going to say to her about why he was on the run, and why he wanted Ayme to stay with her. But he got a reprieve while the women chatted happily with each other and Marjan fixed up a bedroom for Ayme and the baby. Cici was being fussy and his sister helped quiet her with a practiced touch.

"You do that as easily as David does," Ayme told her with admiration as she watched.

"Oh, we all grew up taking care of babies. I sometimes think my whole life has been nothing but babies, from beginning to end."

David coughed discreetly. "There were those years at the Sorbonne."

Marjan grinned "Yes, but we don't talk about those." She rolled her eyes. "Massive waste of time."

David raised an eyebrow. "Didn't you have fun?"

Marjan gave him a look. "Fun is overrated. It often leaves behind a large mess that is very hard to clean up." She turned to Ayme. "You'll want your baby with you, won't you?"

"Oh! Of course."

"We still have a little crib that will be perfect."

She gave them both some soup and sent Ayme, who looked dead on her feet, off to bed. Then she turned to her brother.

"It's not her baby, is it?"

David smiled, waving a soup spoon at her. "You could tell that quickly?"

She nodded. "It wasn't just the fact that she doesn't have a smooth way of caring for her. There was something in the way she looked at the child." she shrugged. "That total depth of feeling just wasn't there."

David nodded slowly. "You're right. But she's actually

a lot better at hiding it than she was when she first burst into my life."

"Oh?"

"At that point she was practically holding the poor thing by one leg."

Marjan laughed. "She was claiming the baby was hers?"

"Yes. But when she constantly referred to a book on child care I knew pretty quickly that she was a fraud."

Marjan frowned. "That's a harsh word to use, don't you think?

"You're right," he said ruefully. "Fake is much more accurate."

Marjan laughed. "Are you going to tell me the story? Or do I just have to wait and read about it in the papers?"

He looked at her ruefully, not sure how much he should tell her.

"Maybe we could start with this—just tell me where you two are headed."

"We're not 'you two'," he said defensively. "We're not a couple."

"No?"

"No. I'm going to Italy. And she's..." He sighed. "I was hoping she could stay with you for a few days."

"Of course." She nodded wisely. "I just read in the paper about the last of the old Ambrian royal family dying. Thaddeus, isn't it? I saw that his memorial service is scheduled to be held in Italy."

David stared at her. "Interesting," he said carefully.

"Yes." Her smile was guileless. "Will you be going to that?" she asked.

David's heart was beating a little harder.

"Why do you ask?" he said.

"No reason." She rose. "Would you like some more soup?" she asked him with a smile.

He didn't answer. He stared at her for a long moment. "How did you know?" he asked at last.

CHAPTER NINE

"OH, DAVID." Marjan ruffled his hair affectionately. "I've long had my own ideas about who you are and why you came to live with us in the middle of the night so long ago."

He stared at her. He'd never known she knew. "I hope you keep those ideas to yourself."

"Oh, I will. I understand the danger." She sat down next to him and reached out to hold his hand. "I figured it out years ago. Remember the summer you were fifteen? Suddenly you were too busy reading to go for a nice bicycle ride by the canals as we used to. You were always with your nose in a book, like you were possessed. I couldn't understand why, so I looked into what you were reading. Ambria. That funny little island country almost nobody knows anything about. But you were crazy for the place, and I was jealous. My buddy was hooked on something new and leaving me behind."

He squeezed her hand and she smiled at him.

"So I started reading about it, too, and I found information about the lost princes. The dates matched the time when you came to live with us. Then I looked at pictures of the royal family." She shook her head, smiling at him. "Then I knew. It was such a great story. My brother, the prince."

He sighed. "Do the others know?"

She shook her head. "I don't think so. I don't think of any of them ever stopped to wonder why you were with us or where you came from, or why a family who already had five children and more on the way would want another one. They just assumed your family were close friends with our parents and we took you in when you needed us to." She laughed softly.

"Do you remember? We spent long summer evenings talking about what was and what could be. I knew there was something more to you than mere happenstance. Besides, I remembered that night you arrived, everyone whispering and acting like something very scary was about to happen." She nodded. "So when I read about that death, I thought you might be going to Italy for the memorial service. I would think it is time for you to take up the cause."

"Are we going to Italy?" Ayme's voice cut into the kitchen's warmth.

They both jumped, realizing Ayme had come into the room behind them. David quickly scanned her face, looking for evidence that she might have heard more than he would want her to. But her eyes were clear. He didn't think she'd heard anything much.

"I have to go to Italy," he told her. "Marjan has said that you can stay here until I get back."

Her eyes suddenly filled with tragedy, imploring him. "Oh, no," she said softly. "But we haven't found that Darius person yet."

He got up from his chair and went to her, reaching

out to take both her hands. She was dressed in a long white nightgown Marjan had loaned her and she looked like an angel. A lump rose in his throat. She was so beautiful, it made his heart hurt.

"We'll talk about it tomorrow," he told her. "Get some sleep. Your eyes are like bruises on your face, they're so dark."

She searched his eyes, then nodded. "All right," she said. "I just came out to get Cici's warmed bottle, but…"

"Here it is," Marjan said, handing it to her. "Good night, Ayme. Let me know if you need anything else."

Ayme gave her a wavering smile. "Good night. And thank you so much."

She gave David one last look and turned to go.

Marjan looked at David's face and her eyes got very round. She nodded knowingly. "Not a couple?" she murmured.

But he was watching Ayme leave and he didn't seem to hear her.

Ayme fed Cici, put her back into her cute little crib and slipped back into the huge fluffy bed. It felt warm and luxurious. Maybe if she just closed her eyes and let herself go limp she would fall asleep right away—and not have to think.

She tried it. It didn't work.

Her eyes shot open and she stared into the darkness. But she wasn't going to think about Sam or her parents. She would never sleep if she let that happen. Better to think about David. She snuggled down into the covers and closed her eyes and imagined David in the bed with her. She was asleep in no time.

* * *

The next day dawned a bit blustery. David made a careful survey of the area from his window on the second floor, but he didn't see any sign of surveillance activities anywhere in the neighborhood. Ayme and Cici came out looking fresh and rested and Marjan cooked them all a wonderful breakfast.

Ayme and David lingered over coffee.

David was trying once again to figure out what had started this race across the continent, and why he'd suddenly known he was in danger and had to flee. Was it really Ayme showing up the way she had? Or the phone call in the night? Or just that it was time to leave for Italy and the sense of a gathering storm had become his reality?

"Have you tried to call that man in Dallas?" he asked her.

She shook her head.

"Has anyone tried to call you?"

She gave him a crooked smile. "How would I know? You made me turn my phone off."

"Check your voice mail," he said.

She checked, but there was nothing. Just the absence of the usual cheery greeting she could expect daily from her mother—a lump formed in her throat, but she shook it off.

He pulled out a leather case that had four cell phones in neat pockets and took a moment to choose one.

"Why do you have so many phones?" she asked.

"Just in case. I like to be prepared." He set a phone up and looked at her. "Okay, give me the number."

"What number?"

"That Carl guy. I want to check him out."

She opened her own phone again and retrieved it,

reading it off to him while he clicked the numbers in. In a moment, there was a snap and a voice answered.

"You've reached the number for Euro Imports. Mr. Heissman is out at the moment. Please leave your name and number so that he may call you back. Thank you for calling Euro Imports."

"Euro Imports," he muttered, getting out his laptop and going on the Internet. There it was. It seemed to be legit.

He looked at Ayme who had been watching all this with interest.

"I guess your friend Carl is at least a real business-man in Dallas," he said. "So if that was him calling the other night, maybe it wasn't such a threatening call after all."

She nodded.

"Or maybe it was something else entirely." He gave her his best Humphrey Bogart impression. "You just never know. The problems of three little people like us don't matter a hill of beans in this crazy world."

She laughed, warmed to think he was talking about the very three people she was thinking of. It almost made it seem like they were a family of sorts.

They finished up their coffee and David asked his sister to watch Cici for an hour so that he could take Ayme along on a pilgrimage of sorts. He wanted to see if old Meneer Garvora, the man who had taught him some of the fundamentals about Ambria, still lived in the area.

They set off down the lane between hedgerows and David told her how the old man had caught him fishing in a landowner's fishpond one day when he was about ten, and as punishment, he'd made him read a book about Ambria and come by to give him a report.

"I have no idea how he knew about my ties to that country, or if he even did know. But he insisted I learn a lot about the place. I owe him a debt of gratitude for that."

He realized now how much the old man had husbanded the flame in him, making sure it didn't go out in the cold wind of international apathy. How had he known how important that would be to David's future?

"I wish someone had taught me a thing or two," Ayme said in response.

He looked over at her and smiled. "I'll teach you everything you need to know," he said.

But she gave him a baleful look and he realized she was brooding about his plan to leave her with his sister.

They reached the little cottage where David's mentor had lived, but the place seemed a bit deserted.

"This looks like a place where hobbits might live," Ayme noted. "Or maybe the seven dwarves."

David knocked on the door but there was no answer. Walking about in the garden, they found a stone bench and sat together on it, gazing into a small pond and enjoying the morning sunshine, and he told Ayme about some of the lessons the old man had given him when he was a boy.

Memory was a strange thing. Now that he'd opened his mind to that past, a lot came flooding in that he hadn't thought of in years. He especially remembered how lost and lonely he'd felt as he tried to make sense of his situation. He'd spent years wondering about his family, wondering what had happened to them.

At one point in his childhood, he'd asked his foster mother. Neither of this second set of parents ever brought up the fact that he was an addition to their thriving nest. They treated him as though he'd come the same way the others had come, and looking back now, he was grateful. But at the time, it made it hard to bring up the subject of his old life. He felt as though he was betraying their kindness in a way. Still, he had to find out whatever he could.

When he'd finally built up the courage to ask, his foster mother had looked sad and pulled him onto her lap and given him a hug. She told him how sorry she was for the tragedies in his life. She gave him sympathy and a tear or two. But what she didn't give him was the truth.

Maybe she didn't know anything else. He realized that now. But at the time, he'd resented the lack of information. He'd felt as though he had to operate blind in a seeing world. He wanted to know about his siblings. He wanted to know what his parents had been like. He had a thousand questions and his foster parents gave him sympathy but not much else.

As he grew older he tried doing research on his own, but he couldn't find much. Most of the world seemed to assume that his entire family had been wiped out in the rebellion, but since he knew different, he didn't take that seriously. He knew there was hope that more royals had survived. Still, he was always aware, just as he'd been aware that dark, stormy night, that the wrong move or a careless word could bring on disaster.

And then he had been found by Meneer Garvora. The old man, in his crusty way, had opened up the world of

Ambria to him. Looking back, he realized now what a resource he had been.

"So he gave you what your new parents just couldn't," Ayme noted. "How lucky that you had him in your life."

He nodded. "My adoptive parents were very nice to me. I thoroughly appreciate all they did for me. And I've had a nice career working for my father's company." His gaze clouded. "But they were never my real parents the way yours seem to have been with you—we never had that special closeness." He shrugged. "Maybe it was because I could still remember my birth parents, and that made it more difficult to attach to new ones. But it was also because there were just so darn many of us kids, it was pretty hard to get much individual attention."

Ayme sighed. "I had all the attention in the world. I was the fair-haired child and I enjoyed every moment of it. Analyzing it now, I can see that their joy in my accomplishments pushed Sam to the sidelines, and I regret it so much."

Tears shimmered in her eyes. David reached out and put an arm around her shoulders, pulling her close. She turned her face up to his and he kissed her softly on the lips.

She smiled. "I like you," she said softly.

He'd only meant to comfort her. He only wanted to shield her from pain. But when she looked up at him and said that so sweetly, he lost all sense of reality in one fell swoop.

He wanted to speak, but his throat was too choked for him to say anything. He more than liked her. He wanted her, needed her, felt an overpowering urge to take her in his arms and kiss her lips and kiss her breasts and make her feel his desire until she was ready to accept him, body and soul.

The thought of taking her body with his set up an ache and a throbbing in him that threatened to blow away all his inhibitions. He was all need, all desire, all urgent hunger. He felt, for just a moment, like a wolf who'd caught sight of the prey that destiny had been saving just for him—how could he be denied?

He took her face in his hands and saw acceptance in her eyes. He could hardly breathe, and his heart was beating so hard he didn't hear the sound of the back gate opening until a voice called out, "Who's here?"

He froze. His body rebelled. Closing his eyes, he forced himself back into a sense of calm, and as he did Ayme slipped from his hands, rising to meet the elderly woman coming around the corner.

"Well, hello," she said. "I've just come to pick up the mail from the box."

David rose as well, feeling like a man who had just avoided the pit of stark, raving madness. He was breathing hard, but he managed to smile and ask "Doesn't Meneer Garvora live here anymore?"

"Oh, certainly, he still lives here just as he has for thirty years," she responded in a kindly manner. "But he's gone on a trip right now. First time I've known him to go anywhere for years and years. He said he might be gone for quite some time." She waved an arm expansively. "I'm watering his pots for him while he's gone."

"I see. I'm sorry to have missed him." Turning, he looked down into Ayme's clear brown eyes. There was a question in them. And why not? What he'd almost done was insane and she was wondering whether he should be committed, no doubt. Internally he groaned. He was going to have to control himself better if he didn't want to bring down the whole house of cards on his own head.

Man up! he told himself silently. *Think of Ambria. Think of Monte.*

"Yes," the lady was saying. "Aren't you one of the Dykstra clan? I seem to remember seeing you visiting here years ago. Am I right?"

"You're right. Meneer Garvora gave me some important geography lessons in the old days. I just wanted to come by and thank him for that."

"I'll tell him you came by."

They started to go and David turned back. "By the way, did he say where he was going?"

"Yes, of course. He went to Italy."

David's eyebrows rose at that news. Thanking the woman, he nodded to Ayme and they started back down the path to the farmhouse.

"Hmm," Ayme said, noting his reaction to hearing his old mentor's destination. "Are we going to Italy, too?" she asked, just a bit archly.

He growled but didn't really answer.

"If I could just find this Darius person," she murmured.

He looked at her and frowned. "Listen, we need to talk about that." He hesitated, but there was no time like the present. "You do realize it is not very likely he was ever planning to marry your sister."

"Oh, I know that." She waved his statement away. "Knowing Sam, I doubt she was ever planning to marry him." She smiled sadly, remembering her sister. "Sam wasn't one to yearn for marriage. In fact, she wasn't one to stick with one man for more than a weekend."

He made a face. "Ouch."

"Well might you say that." She nodded, remembering the painful past. "I'm expecting him to be a sort of male version of Sam, if you know what I mean." She gazed at him earnestly as they walked along. "I just think he has a right to know about Cici and she has a right to the chance that her Dad might want her."

He winced. He was only just beginning to realize how hard this was all going to be. "I know. It's been bothering me, too."

"I don't know how much you can blame him. I mean I'm sure he's the sort of man who has women throwing themselves at him constantly. Being a handsome young and eligible prince and all."

He had to give her that. He nodded with a half smile he couldn't hold back. "Of course he does. But that doesn't mean he has to accept them, does it? Not if he has any integrity."

She gave him a bemused smile. "Celebrities with integrity? I'm sure there are a few, but…" She shrugged. "Hey, I've had men throw themselves at me all my life. Some seem to think I do have certain charms."

His sideways glance was warm. "I'll second that emotion."

She felt a glow of pleasure but she didn't want to lose her equilibrium. "But I would never let it go to my head. That way lies the pit, and once you fall over the edge, you're done for."

He grinned at her melodramatic tone. But then his grin faded as he remembered how he'd almost lost control just a half hour before. He hadn't even known it was possible. He'd never felt anything like that before, so strong, so overwhelming, so irresistible. It was almost scary—his own private "pit."

"So anyway, I think I should give him a chance to make a case for himself. Mostly for Cici's sake."

He had to admire her for that. If only he wasn't pretty sure that this guy was a rat, and maybe even needed exterminating.

Something stopped him just before they got back within sight of his sister's house. Some natural-born instinct for survival, perhaps. Whatever it was, it told him right away that danger lurked, and he had Ayme follow him as they stayed behind the bushes and traveled down along the hedge at the edge of the canal instead of walking in on the road. They kept out of sight and sneaked in through the back gate, surprising Marjan in the kitchen.

"Oh, I'm so glad you came in that way," she said as soon as she saw them. "I've just heard from my friend Tilly Weil that there is a man watching the house. He hangs out in that little stand of trees over there, across the way, pretending to be a bird watcher."

David went to the window, standing to the side. "How long has he been there?" he asked.

"Tilly thought he was there early this morning, then seemed to go have breakfast somewhere and is now back, binoculars in hand. So you see, you didn't get away with your ride in the hay wagon."

"Maybe," David said. "And maybe he's just watching my sister's house in case I might show up there. You can't tell." He looked at Ayme. "But I'd better go."

Ayme turned to look at him, her eyes huge. He felt

an ache in his heart. It was going to be hard to leave her behind.

"First of all," his sister said, "I know you're going to be anxious to go, but from what we've seen, I think you're right, that they don't know for sure whether you are here or not. And I say you wait until morning. If you do that, you'll have a place to stay tonight, and tomorrow I may have a way to get you out of here completely unseen by the outside world."

David thought for a moment. She had a point. If they left now, they would just have to find another place to stay for the night and it was getting late for that.

"All right," he said at last. "We'll go in the morning. Early."

"Ayme, I hope you'll be staying here with me," Marjan said, trying to help David do the right thing. She turned to him. "She'll be a big help, and at the same time I could teach her some practical things about babies."

He studied his sister's pleasant face for a moment, feeling a warmth for her he didn't feel for many other people. But he couldn't look at Ayme. He knew she was holding her breath, waiting to see what he would say.

Various and sundry thoughts ranged through his head as he stood there, thoughts about his brother's plan to match him up with the woman who was perfect princess material, about how his brother had warned him against getting entangled with Ayme, about how much easier it would be to sneak around on his own if she stayed behind. He had to keep his eye on the prize. He knew that. Ayme being with him tended to diffuse his focus at times.

His head knew all these things and agreed with them.

But his heart and soul had other ideas. He couldn't keep her with him forever, but he wanted her close right now. He needed her. Why? He wasn't ready to verbalize that just yet.

But he also wanted to make sure she was protected. For now. Not for always—that was impossible. But for now. For now.

He'd made up his mind. He was taking her to Italy with him. Monte wasn't going to like it, but he didn't care. Monte wasn't king yet.

"Thank you for your offer, Marjan. I appreciate it and love you for it. But I can't take you up on it. Ayme has to come with me."

Ayme's heart leaped in her chest. Yes!

Marjan's smile was understanding. "Well, then, how about the baby? You can leave her here. I'll take care of her. You need to be able to slide through the world without the baggage a baby entails."

Ayme's heart was beating as fast as a bird's, making her feel faint. She held her breath. Deep inside, she knew there was no way she would ever leave this helpless little baby behind. But what would David say?

He turned slowly. He looked at her and then he looked at Cici.

"That's up to Ayme," he said, then glanced at her. "She would be safe here," he suggested. "What do you say?"

She searched his gaze, looking for clues as to what he really thought. Did he want the freedom that being without the baby would bring? She could understand that he might. But she couldn't accept it. She needed Cici to come with them.

She drew in a deep breath. She was going to insist,

even if that meant David decided to have her stay instead of go. That was the way it had to be. She closed her eyes and said a little prayer.

Then she opened them and said, loud and clear, "Cici needs to go with us. That's where she belongs."

David smiled. "Good," he said firmly. "Thank you, Marjan, but we'll keep Cici with us."

Ayme felt a glow of happiness in her chest. It seemed to be settling right where her heart should be. She raced off to pack for the trip.

They had a lovely dinner. Ayme helped Marjan cook it, stopping to tend to Cici in between her duties. They ate heartily and laughed a lot. That night, they slept well.

When they were ready to go, they found that Marjan had set up a special plan for them.

"Okay, Mari. Tell me. What's your idea?" David asked her.

"Here's the scenario. You said you wanted to throw them off by going back to where you left the car and taking it."

"Yes."

Marjan frowned. "Won't they know?"

He shrugged. "I doubt it. They'll already have checked it out for any information they could use. There would be no reason for them to keep watch on it when they think we've abandoned it."

Marjan nodded, but suggested, "You could take my car."

"Thanks, Mari, but they probably have it pegged too, just in case. I think my idea is the best."

She nodded again, thinking. "All right then. Now, as for my plan, my friend Gretja takes her canal boat in to town every other morning. Today she is stopping by in half an hour to pick up my pies to take to the Cheese Fair. How would you like to ride back to town in a canal boat?"

David was all smiles. "That would be perfect."

"Good." She gave him a hug, then turned to Ayme and did the same. "I want you both to be safe and happy. So be careful!"

Forty minutes later they were on Gretja's canal boat, tucked away inside the little open cabin in a place where no one could see them from the shore. Gretja enjoyed the whole event more than anyone. As they were skimming along the waterway, the older woman grinned at them from above, her eyes sparkling as though she were carrying smugglers out of Kashmir.

"Oh, isn't this fun? I'm trying not to move my lips when I talk so they can't see me. Just in case anyone should be watching from the side, you know. I think I'll pretend to be singing. Yes, that should work just fine. Don't you think so?"

They humored her. The trip didn't take long, but it was fun while it lasted. They thanked her profusely when she dropped them off in town, choosing a crowded dock where they wouldn't be noticed. A few minutes later they were back in David's "incognito" car and driving toward France.

"I don't know how much more of this craziness I can take," Ayme said as she settled in and began to give Cici her bottle. "I'm just a stay-at-home girl from Dallas. I'm not used to all these shenanigans."

"Don't forget that semester in Japan," he reminded her sardonically.

"Well, yes, there was that." Her eyes narrowed as she

thought that over. "But we had escorts and chaperones everywhere we went. It was very controlled. Here I feel like I keep getting aboard a crazy train that's running wild. What if it goes off the tracks?"

He watched her, his eyes slightly hooded in a way she considered exceptionally sexy.

"Don't worry. You've got me to catch you if you fall off."

"Do I?"

He was kidding but she smiled at him anyway. At the same time, she wished she could ask him: *"But who are you?"*

She didn't ask it aloud, but it was always there in the back of her mind. She knew there was more to him than he was giving her. She just didn't know what it was.

She had caught a word or two between David and his sister, but she was in the dark. Bottom line, she didn't really care. She just wanted to be with David. She'd had to throw caution to the wind to go with him in the first place, and that was what she was doing again.

Was she falling in love with the man? How could she tell when she didn't really know who he was. She certainly had a pretty strong crush, stronger than any attachment she'd ever felt for any man—or boy— before. Was that love? She needed more information. Finally, she screwed up her courage and asked him the question.

"David, when are you going to tell me who you really are?" she asked, watching closely for his reaction.

His gaze flickered her way and she had the distinct impression he was looking to see just how much she thought she knew. What did that mean?

"I mean, I know most of the world thinks you're a

Dutchman named David Dykstra, but you're really not him at all. So who are you?"

"No, Ayme, you've got that wrong," he said with exaggerated patience. "I really am David Dykstra. It's just that I'm someone else, as well."

"Someone Ambrian."

"Right."

"And what is that someone's name?"

He shook his head and didn't look her way. "Later."

"Oh!" She growled. "I hate that answer."

"It's the only answer I can give right now."

"It's not acceptable." She waited and when he didn't elaborate, she added, "When is later, anyway?"

He glared at her, not smiling. "I'll let you know when I feel I can."

"Why can't you do it right now?"

"Ayme…"

She held up a hand. "I know, I know, it's too dangerous."

"Well, it is. I don't want you to get hurt because you know too much."

"Sure." Her mouth twisted cynically. "They could come and kidnap me. Where would I be then? They might put me on the rack and pull me apart until my bones snap." She punched a fist into the upholstery. "But I'll never talk. I'll say, 'No, you blackguards, you won't get anything out of me!'"

She sighed, dropping the phony accent. "Or I could tell them everything I know, which is more likely. So I understand why you won't tell me. You think I'll fold under pressure." She turned to give him a knowing look. "But what happens when I figure it out for myself? Then what? Huh?"

"You're making jokes, Ayme," he said calmly. "But your being tortured for information is no laughing matter. It could happen." He frowned. "Which makes me wonder why I let you come along."

"Okay," she said quickly. "Let's stop speculating. I won't beg for information anymore. I swear."

He looked at her earnest face and laughed. "Liar," he said softly.

"Okay, then how about this old chestnut? Where are we really going?"

"To Piasa, Italy. My uncle died. I need to attend his memorial service."

"Oh."

Wow. That was a lot more than she'd expected and it took her a moment of two to digest it.

"Your Ambrian uncle?" she asked.

He nodded.

She opened her mouth to ask more about that but he silenced her with a quick oath.

"No more, Ayme," he said. "That's enough for now."

"Okay." Suddenly, she remembered something.

"I forgot to tell you. I saw the white-haired man again."

His head turned quickly. "What? Where?"

"When we were transferring from the canal boat to the car. I couldn't warn you because we were sort of occupied at the time, the way we were sneaking around to find the car. But I saw him, or somebody who looked just like him, going into a store across the square. I don't think he saw us."

"Damn." He thought for a moment, then shook his head. "Okay, hang on."

Soon they were flying down the road at breakneck speed and Ayme was hanging on for dear life. She took a few minutes of this, then called out, "Hey, slow down. They can drive fast, too. You're not going to avoid them this way."

He let up a bit on the speed, but they were still going too fast. "You're right," he said. "I just wanted to feel like I was doing something, making some progress."

"With a little bit of luck, they don't know where we are and won't be coming up behind us," she said. "You never know." She sighed. "I never realized before how much of what happens to you in life is just based on dumb, blind luck."

He nodded, slowing even more. "Sure, to some extent. But there's also grit and determination and how much you're willing to put into life."

"One would hope. I've always used that as my template. Work hard and ye shall reap the rewards thereof, or something like that. But..." She threw up her hands. "Look at how much luck smoothed the way for me in life. I was adopted by a wonderful set of parents who adored me and did so well for me. What if I'd ended up with some other people? I was so lucky to get the Sommerses."

"So lucky, it almost balanced out the bad luck of losing your birth parents to begin with," he noted dryly.

"You're right." She frowned. "There's as much bad luck as there is good, isn't there?"

"At least as much."

She thought for a long moment, then ventured a look his way. "That last day in Dallas, I was alone with Cici. She slept all day. I was terrified she would wake up and

I would have to hold her. I had no clue what to do with babies. My parents had raced off to find Sam and bring her home without telling me anything except, 'take care of Cici.'" She sighed.

"If only Sam hadn't run away. If only my parents hadn't found out so quickly where she'd gone. If only… If only…" She closed her eyes for a moment, then opened them again.

"But when I opened the front door and found a policeman standing there, I knew. Right away, I knew. It was like the end of the world had come to my door. The end of my world, for sure."

He peered at her sideways, wondering if she was finally going to tell him about her parents' deaths.

"But consider this," she went on. "I was in shock, and it was just luck that I was so overcome that I didn't think to mention Cici to them. If I'd had her out at the time, or if she'd begun to cry, I would have remembered to tell them about her. They probably would have taken her away. Instead, there I was with Sam's baby and no family left."

There it was. He waited, poised. No family left. Maybe now she would go on and tell him about her parents. He looked at her, waiting for her to amplify. But she was staring out the window, brooding, so he coaxed her to continue.

"So that was bad luck?"

"No. No, not really. When I was able to think straight again, I realized Cici was now my responsibility. I couldn't let some social agency take her. I had to find her father."

He shrugged. "Perhaps if you'd told the authorities about her, *they* would have found her father."

"Maybe. But because of Sam's lifestyle and the crazy things she did, I have a feeling there would have been entanglements and problems. And delays. And red tape. No, I knew from the beginning it would be better if I could find a way to take care of it myself. Besides, I needed…" Her voice faded away.

He glanced at her. "Needed what?"

"Nothing." She cleared her throat. She'd needed to have something to do, somewhere to go, so that she wouldn't have to deal with her parents' deaths. "I was talking about Cici. At first, I didn't know anything about babies. My main concern was just to get her to someone who could take care of her and give her the love she needed. And that was why I dashed over here as soon as I found someone I could go to—and that was you."

"And here you are."

"Look at the blind dumb luck in you turning out to be the sort of man you are." She was looking at him with unabashed affection. "You actually cared. You gave me shelter from the storm."

"Some shelter," he said gruffly. "I threw you into a car and we've been racing across Europe ever since."

There was a quivering thread of passion in her voice when she said, "You made all the difference."

He looked away, steeling himself. He knew what was happening here. Her words were reaching into his heart and soul and touching his emotions like they'd never been touched before. If he wasn't careful, he was going to fall for it.

Not that she was trying to fool him. She wasn't. It was obvious that she was totally sincere. But Ayme's sincerity was already messing with his mind and he knew how much he already cared about her. He couldn't afford any more. If he let her into the secret places where his real feelings lay buried, he'd be done for.

CHAPTER TEN

DAVID had always known he was royal. He wasn't Monte. Monte would probably have been king right now if they were back in Ambria where they belonged. He was glad that responsibility was his older brother's and not his. Still, he knew if anything happened to Monte, he would be more than ready to take his place. It was the natural order of things.

Sometimes he wondered why he seemed to know this so instinctively. He hadn't had a family to pound these things into him, like most royals would have. He didn't have years and years of tutors teaching him about his place, years and years of servants treating him like he really was someone special. But he knew anyway. He knew it was both a special advantage and a special danger—as well as a responsibility.

"Uneasy lies the head that wears a crown," as Shakespeare wrote so long ago. He accepted that. It was part of the role as he'd always envisioned it. But that didn't mean it was a simple thing to deal with.

And romance certainly complicated matters. For a long time he'd assumed that casual romance came with the territory. It seemed all the royals he read about in the gossip papers were naturally promiscuous. He'd given that a try himself, but he hadn't really taken to it. Something in him seemed to be searching for that special someone who would complete his life.

Where he had gotten such a mundane, ordinary idea he wasn't sure. Maybe it had to do with the good, solid Dutch family that had raised him with morals and values that he couldn't seem to shake, even if he'd wanted to. Maybe it was something more basic. He wasn't sure, he only knew it made it hard to treat love as casually as people seemed to expect.

And now there was Ayme.

Wait. Why had he thought of that? What did this woman who had appeared out of nowhere and parked herself and her baby in his apartment have to do with anything? He wasn't falling in love with her. Of course he wasn't because that would be nuts.

"Where are we going next?"

He smiled. Her questions didn't even annoy him anymore. He expected them, like a parent expected the inevitable "Are we there yet?".

"As I told you, our ultimate destination is in Italy," he said to her.

"Are we going through Paris?" she asked hopefully.

"No. We're sticking to the back roads."

"Oh." Her disappointment was obvious. "I've always wanted to sip a glass of wine in a Parisian café," she said, her head tilted dreamily. "Preferably a sidewalk café. With a man playing an accordion and a woman singing torch songs in the background."

"Edith Piaf, no doubt."

"If possible." She grinned at him. "Why not?"

"I don't think she's around anymore."

"I know. Only in dreams."

He looked at her. More than anything, he wanted her to be happy.

"We'll do it," he said softly.

She looked at him in surprise. "But we're in a hurry."

He nodded. "We can't go to Paris. But don't worry. I'll find us a sidewalk café. Just have faith."

"I've got nothing but faith in you," she told him happily.

He took one look at her face and pulled over to the side of the road. In one smooth move, he had his arms around her and was kissing the heck out of her. She kissed him back once she was over her surprise. And when he pulled away, he touched her cheek and said, softly, "I thought you needed kissing."

She nodded. "You were right. I did."

He grinned and turned back to the wheel. They were back on the road in no time at all.

It was a couple of hours later when he turned onto a rutted road and told her what their next stop would be.

"We'll find you that sidewalk café very soon," he said. "But right now, I want you to see Ambria."

"Ambria!" She sat up straighter. Suddenly she was terrified.

"Yes. Ambria."

She swallowed a sudden lump in her throat. "How am I going to do that?"

"Under the right conditions, you can see her from the shore. I've done it. It's just a few miles ahead."

She pulled her arms in tightly around her chest and looked worried. "I'm not sure I want to see Ambria."

He gazed at her levelly. "Why not?"

"I...I don't know. I'm afraid it will change things."

He looked out the window and frowned, thinking. "You may be right," he said at last. "But I think you should see it, anyway."

She was silent for a long time and he didn't push her. Finally she said, "I'll do it, as long as you stay with me."

"Of course." He looked at her again. "Don't forget, you were born there. Deep down, you're Ambrian."

That didn't sit well with her. "I'm an American," she told him. "And I'm a Texan. And maybe I'm an Ambrian, too. But I don't feel it."

He nodded and his smile was pure affection. "That's why I'm taking you there."

She took in that affection like a flower took in sunshine. And in her own way, she bloomed a little. "Okay. I'll try to see what you want me to see. I'll try to like it."

"That's all I ask."

She gave a little hiccup of a laugh. "Just remember," she said. "In the immortal words of the Supremes, you can't hurry love."

He nodded. He knew what she meant. "Even love of country."

"Exactly."

They stopped along the way to get a couple of cold lemonades and then to let Ayme give Cici a bottle. The baby wanted to play so the stop took longer than they had expected. It was early afternoon by the time they got to the seashore.

What Ayme saw was unimpressive. If she looked carefully, she could just make out a sort of somber lump of land hidden behind a wall of melancholy fog. The entire aspect was grim and cheerless, like a prison off shore. She looked at David, hoping he couldn't read her disappointment in her face. But he was staring out at it, so she went back to staring, too.

As they watched, the clouds began to part above the gloomy, fog-shrouded island nation. Ayme reached out and took David's hand but she didn't meet his gaze. Instead, she was staring straight out to sea.

They watched for a long time. Eventually, the sun broke through and shafts of silver-gold sunlight shot down, illuminating the place. The fog lifted and there it was. And suddenly, she was transfixed. She'd never seen anything so beautiful before.

"That's Ambria?" she asked, breathless.

"That's Ambria," he said, satisfaction in his voice. "I haven't been there since I was six years old but it lives in my heart every day."

She shook her head and looked back. The vision was so brilliant, she almost had to shield her eyes.

"It's not in my heart yet," she said, "but it's knocking on the door."

David started talking in a low, vibrant voice. He talked about their Ambrian ancestors, about what it must have been like for their parents, about lives lost and dreams deferred. She listened and took in every word. She began to feel what had been lost. He spoke of how her parents had probably died there, and tears began to well in her eyes.

She wanted to tell him to stop, but somehow she couldn't. He went on and on and she listened, and soon her tears became sobs. He took her into his arms, but he didn't stop talking. And then he mentioned the loss

of her sister, Samantha, and finally, of her adoptive
parents.

She didn't even stop to wonder how he knew about
that. He knew everything, it seemed. He was her everything. She trusted him and she loved him. And finally,
the dam within her let go and she could mourn.

She had a lot to mourn about. Her birth parents, Sam,
her Texas parents. It hardly seemed fair that one young
woman should have to bear the weight of so much suffering on her slender shoulders. And she had avoided
it for a long time. But finally, it was here, and she had
David beside her. She could mourn.

He held her tightly and he rocked her and whispered
comfort in her ear. She clung to him. She needed him.
He was all that was keeping her from being swept away
by a river of grief.

And when her crying was spent and the torrent was
over, she told him about the accident—about how her
parents had found Sam and how Sam had jumped into
the car and driven off, and how her parents had given
chase. And Sam had made a hard turn that had sent her
skidding the wrong way, and her father, unable to stop in
time, had smashed into Sam's car. All three dead from
one stupid accident that shouldn't have happened. And
at first she'd thought she might as well have died with
them. Her life was over.

Things didn't look quite that way any longer, but still,
it was a black cloud that might never leave her.

She wasn't sure what she wanted anymore. In some
ways she felt like her emotions had been tugged in too
many different directions in the past few days. She
couldn't take much more. She'd had it. The only place

she wanted to be right now was in a nice warm bath, with candles set around for good measure.

Back at the car, she drank the rest of the lemonade and kissed Cici and felt a bit revived, and then they were off. David was determined to find a nice sidewalk café for her, and he did just that in the next little town. It was as cute and quaint as she could have asked for and the three of them left the car and sat at a table, and David and Ayme drank wine and ate lovely biscuits. The torch songs were on the radio, but they did just fine. It was wonderful.

And then, Ayme saw the man again, riding past on a bicycle.

"Oh, David, look. The white-haired man."

David spun around. "The man from the first place we stayed?"

"Yes. Did you see him?"

"Yes." He stared down into his wine. "I've seen him before."

"Where? When?"

It was odd how he'd never really remarked on it before, but the man had popped up along the sidelines of his life in the past. Now that she'd pointed him out, he saw that clearly. Was he a threat? How could he take it any other way?

"We've got to get out of here," he said, rising. "We'd better go."

"The car?"

"No. We can't take the car. We'll have to do something else. Come on."

They left the table and began to walk quickly down the street. And then a van drove up beside them and two men jumped out and life became a jumbled, violent mess.

It all happened so fast. The men grabbed David. He struggled, but Ayme saw blood and knew he'd been hit with something. Her first impulse was to stand still and scream at the top of her lungs, but that wouldn't have helped anyone. There was another man getting out of the van and she was pretty sure he would be coming for her next.

David was hurt. She knew it. She couldn't do anything about it, but maybe she could save Cici. She turned and ran as she'd never run before, down between buildings, across railroad tracks, through a yard, over a fence, down an alley, into a field and back between buildings again.

She couldn't breathe. She felt as though there was a stone on her chest. And still she ran, holding Cici as tightly as she dared, adrenaline rushing through her veins. If she could just find some place to hide, a hole in the wall, a little cave, a wooden box, something.

But she ran out of luck before she found it. She was never sure if it was the blow to her head or the cloth soaked with chloroform under her nose that knocked her out, but suddenly there were people at both ends of the alley she'd run down.

"End of the line, little lady," said a burly man, just before they put the cloth over her face and something hit her just above the temple. She was out like a light.

She woke up in a hospital bed. There were voices all around but at first she couldn't focus on what they were saying. She drifted off and when she woke again, she was a bit more alert. A man was sitting beside her bed.

She turned her head to look at him. It was the white-haired man.

She gasped and looked for an escape, but he leaned over the bed with a sweet smile, shaking his head.

"I'm not one of the bad guys, Ayme," he told her. "Believe it or not, I was the one who rescued your little group before the Granvilli thugs could cart you off to Ambria, which seemed to be their objective."

She stared at him. Should she believe him? She scanned the room, which seemed to be a normal hospital room, not some dungeon or hideout. She began to relax.

"David is in a room down the hall. I'm sure you want to know how he is. Well, he's doing fairly well, though his injuries are much more extensive than yours. You have a lump on your head and will probably have a headache for a while, but the doctor says you're doing fine."

"Cici?" she asked, as she reached up to touch the lump he was referring to.

"Not hurt at all. They have her in a crib in the children's ward, but that's only because they don't know what else to do with her right now."

She narrowed her eyes, looking at him. He seemed nice. But then he always had. Could she trust him?

"Who are you?"

He smiled again. "My name doesn't matter. I'm allied with the Ambrian restoration team. We want to restore the royal family to its rightful place on the throne of our country."

"Then, why were you following David everywhere?"

He leaned closer and spoke as though in private.

"The truth is, I've been following David for years, trying to make sure nothing threatened him until he was ready."

"Ready?" She was getting confused again. "Ready for what?"

He smiled. "I see David needs to explain a few things to you. But I'll let him do that." He rose from his chair. "And now that you're awake, I'll go back to David, if you don't mind. Have the nurse contact me if you need anything, my dear." He nodded his head in her direction and left the room.

She stared after him, still not sure what was going on. When the team of men had driven up in the van and they'd been attacked, she'd thought it was exactly what David had been guarding against all this time. At least, from what he'd told her, that was what she assumed.

But the white-haired man had been a part of that threat—hadn't he? Now it seemed David had been wrong about that. But she really didn't understand. How had she let herself get involved, anyway?

She had to get out of here and she had to get Cici out. Rolling out of the bed, she clutched the hospital gown around herself and made her way to the door. She was dizzy, but it wasn't bad enough to stop her. She had to know how David and Cici really were, not just what someone she didn't really trust was telling her.

Up and down the hallway all seemed clear and she started toward the room across the hall. In the third room she checked, there was David. He had a big bandage on his head and appeared to be regaining consciousness. The white-haired man was there. But the strange thing was, he was bowed over from the waist and seemed to be kissing David's hand.

"Your Highness," he was saying. "I'm at your service, always."

She pulled back so that she couldn't be seen and tried to catch her breath.

Your highness? Your highness?

But hadn't she suspected this? Hadn't she known it all along? It all fell together. The pieces just fell into place. David was royal. Of course.

The white-haired man left the room, walking off down the hall without seeing where she was standing, half-hidden by a bank of oxygen tanks. She waited until he was out of sight, then slipped into David's room and approached him.

He looked as though he'd been through a meat grinder. Her heart flipped in her chest as she saw his most obvious wounds.

"Oh, David," she said, reaching for his hand.

He looked up and tried to smile around a swollen lip.

"Hi, Ayme," he said. "Hey, nice little frock you've got on there."

She ignored that. "Are you okay?" she asked anxiously.

"I'm okay. I'm still groggy from pain medication, but once I get that out of my system, I'll be good to go." His smile was bittersweet and his voice was rough. "I didn't protect you very well, did I?"

"What?" She shook her head, then grimaced. It hurt to do that. "I'm just so glad you're not badly injured," she said. "It all happened so fast."

"Yes. Thank God for Bernard and his men."

She looked at him questioningly. "The white-haired man?"

"Yes. He said he'd talked to you."

"Yes."

"Did he tell you how he and his men swooped in and saved my butt?"

"No."

He nodded slightly. "Let's reserve that story for later," he said, obviously starting to lag a bit. "Just be thankful they were there, keeping an eye on the situation. Without them, we'd be..." He let his voice trail off. He didn't really want to speculate right now.

"So, let me get this straight," she was saying. "There were bad guys following us. But there were also good guys following us?"

"That's about it."

And that left the question of why. But she knew that now, didn't she? She studied his face for a moment and then gave him a sad smile.

"You're one of them, aren't you?"

His eyes had been drifting shut, but they opened again. "One of whom?"

"The lost royals." Her heart was hammering in her chest. "Which one are you?"

He closed his eyes and turned away.

"Don't tell me you're Darius. Are you?" She wanted to grab him and shake him, but she knew she couldn't do that. "Are you Cici's father?" she asked, her voice strangled.

He opened his eyes again and looked at her. "No. That I am not."

She shook her head, feeling as though she were drowning in unhappiness. "How do you know?"

"Ayme, I never met Sam. Believe me, I've thought long and hard about it, just to make sure. It's not me."

"But you're Prince Darius. And at the same time, you're looking for him? I don't get it."

He tried to pull up to a seated position, but it was beyond him at this point. "Don't you see? I'm not looking for Darius. I know where he is. I'm looking for the man who's pretending to be me. That's the one we need to find."

"Why is he pretending?"

"Why not? If it helps him with the ladies, why not?"

She lowered her head and thought about that. She had to admit, Sam had been just crazy enough to fall for something like that.

"Of course, there's another theory. He might have been pretending to be Darius in order to try to lure me or any of my siblings who may have survived out of hiding. That's why we've got to find him."

"So either way, he's probably a jerk."

"Looks like."

Her sigh came from the depths of her soul. "And what if he wants Cici? Do I have to give her up to a jerk who might even be a criminal?" She searched his eyes, desperate for a good answer.

But he didn't have one for her. He could barely keep his eyes open. She gave up.

"I'm going to go see if I can get checked out of here," she told him. "I'll be back later."

He didn't answer. He was sound asleep.

A few minutes later she was dressed and ready to leave. Luckily, no one seemed to be paying much attention to her and she'd managed to prepare to check out without having to fill out any forms. All she had to do was find

Cici. She started down the hall, then hesitated. David's room was like a magnet. She wanted to see him one last time. Walking softly, she looked into the room. There was a man she didn't recognize talking to David.

"You've still got the Ambrian girl with you," he was saying.

"Ayme?" David asked groggily.

"Yes. What do you want me to do about her?"

"Do about her?"

"Your brother, the Crown Prince, has asked that you not bring her to Piasa. He has someone he thinks would make a perfect match for you waiting there to meet you and it would be..."

Pulling back, she began to walk on down the hall, pacing quickly, thinking, thinking. Her mind raced with plans. The pain of being cast aside would overwhelm her if she let it. She had to push it away and ignore it for now.

What was she going to do? She had to get out of here and she had to take Cici with her. It was obvious that she would never have David. She had to shut that off, not think about losing him. She had lost so much lately. And then, as though fate had lead her to the right place, there was Cici, alone in a room with only one little crib.

"Oh, my baby!" she cried as she rushed to hold her.

Was that a smile? Yes! Her heart filled with love as she held the child close and murmured sweet things to her. At the same time her mind whirred with ideas of how she could take her away before people asked questions and began to require official forms to be signed. If she could just get her back on a plane to Texas, she would be in a position to make a claim on her. Once she lost control of her here in Europe, there was no telling what would happen next. She might have no chance of ever getting her back.

At the same time, she knew what she was about to do was probably illegal. If she got caught, it could be all over for her. But if she just let Cici slip away, the last thing she loved in this world would be gone. Some choice she had. The pit or the pendulum.

She was going to risk it.

David was on the phone with Monte.

"We found him."

David had to concentrate and be sure he understood. His mind was still fuzzy. "Okay, you've got the guy who was pretending to be me? Is that right?"

"Well, in a manner of speaking. He's dead, has been for a few weeks, but we know who he is."

"Dead? How?"

Monte's voice lowered. "It looks like an assasination. He was shot by a sniper."

"Oh, my God."

"Yes. We assume whoever shot him thought he was you. He'd been using that story about being one of the lost royals to seduce young women off and on for a couple of years. It finally caught up with him."

They were both silent for a moment, taking that in.

Finally, Monte said, "You know what this means, don't you?"

"You tell me."

"This means that, however much we're tempted to say 'aw, forget about it, let's just go on and live our lives like everyone else,' that's not going to work. Because there are people out there who feel threatened by our very existence, and until we find a way to take back our country and get rid of those people, we're in danger. We'll never be safe, and neither will the ones we love."

He was right. David closed his eyes and swore softly. He didn't have a choice. He was Prince Darius of Ambria and he was going to have to deal with it.

"So, I guess I'll see you in Piasa on Friday? You're good to go?"

"Yes. I'll be there."

Monte hesitated. "About this Ayme person," he began.

David was fully awake now. "She'll be there, too," he said firmly. "She's with me."

There was a pause. "You do realize how important this is," Monte reminded him. "Every Ambrian who can make it will be there. This is our time to claim our heritage."

"I understand that, Monte, and I'll be there right beside you. I'll fight to the death for you and for our cause. For our place in history. But I'll be the one to decide on my private life, on what I need and what I don't."

Monte let his breath out in a long sigh. "Okay," he said. "That's your call. But I wish you'd reconsider."

David smiled, thinking of Ayme, thinking of Cici. There would be no problem with them keeping the baby now. "I've gone beyond the point of no return," he told his brother. "Take it or leave it."

"Okay. I'll take it. See you in Italy."

David was fully awake now. He looked around the sterile hospital room.

"Enough of this," he said, ripping the IV out of his arm and easing off the bed. He took it slowly. He was weak and he didn't want to end up on the floor. But he was going to find Ayme if it killed him.

He found his clothes and put them on, then headed out into the hallway. He knew that finding Cici would be the key to Ayme's location, and he knew where Cici had been put. He passed three separate nurses and a doctor, each of whom gave him curious looks, but didn't try to stop him. But when he arrived at his destination, the room was empty.

Alarm shot through him. If she'd already left, would he be able to find her again? He looked out the window. From the third story where he was, he could see Ayme heading down the walkway, Cici in her arms.

He couldn't run, but he moved faster than he would have thought possible and caught up to her before she got off the grounds.

"What are you doing?" he called to her as he got close.

She whirled, holding Cici to her chest. "Uh…uh…" Her eyes were huge and she looked guilty as hell.

"You're kidnapping Cici," he said, trying to keep the amusement hidden in his eyes. "Do you know you could be put in prison for something like that?"

"I'm not!" She gasped. "Oh, no. That's not what I'm doing." Her eyes filled with tears. "Oh, David," she wailed.

"Ayme, darling," he said, laughing as he pulled her into his arms. "Why are you running away?"

She gazed up at him, tears streaming down her face. "David, I've lost everything I ever loved. And now I've lost you. I can't bear to lose Cici, too."

He looked down into her pretty face. "Why do you think you've lost me?"

"You're royal. I...I'm not from that world."

"Neither am I. Not really. I didn't grow up preparing to be royal." He dropped a kiss on her nose. "Oh, Ayme, I want you with me. We can learn about being royal together."

"But, Cici..."

He pulled back and got serious. "They found Cici's father. I'm afraid he's dead."

Quickly, he told her what Monte had told him.

"So your search is over." He touched her cheek. "But I'm hoping our journey together has just begun."

She searched his gaze. "Do you mean that?"

"With all my heart."

"Oh, David!"

He kissed her, then pulled back.

"Come on. Let's get a cab and find a nice hotel."

"But, don't we need to tell the hospital?"

"Don't worry about it. This is the good side of being royal. We have people who take care of these little details for us."

"Like the white-haired man?"

"His name is Bernard. Get used to it. I have a feeling we'll be seeing a lot of him."

"Really?"

"And that Carl Heissman who first sent you to me? He's an associate of Bernard's. He wasn't sure if Sam's claim that Prince Darius was Cici's father would hold up, but he thought it best to send you to me to find out. You see, there are wheels within wheels. I'm sure we don't know the half of it yet."

He sobered.

"Do you understand?" he asked her. "I love you, Ayme. I want to marry you. But I don't want to sugarcoat this. It's something you're going to have to consider going forward. I want you with me, but you have to be willing to take the risks involved."

She shook her head, ready to be supremely happy, but warned against it by the tone of his voice. "What are you talking about?"

"We're about to start a major push on Ambria to win our country back. If we go ahead with it, there will likely be fighting. There will be danger. There may be dying. You will be risking a lot just by being associated with me. You must think this through and decide if it's worth it."

Reaching up, she flattened her hand against the plane of his handsome face. "David, my life was over until I met you. Now it's about to begin again. I'll risk it. I'll risk anything to be with you."

He kissed her again. After all these years of wondering what the big deal about love was, it seemed like a miracle that he had found a woman he couldn't live without, a woman he had to spend his life with.

"We'll be together."

"And Cici?"

As if on cue, the baby gurgled happily. They looked at each other and laughed.

"I think she'll probably be with us, too."

Ayme sighed with pure happiness, looking down at the child she'd come to love with all her heart.

"Good. Let's go to Italy."

MILLS & BOON

OCTOBER 2010 HARDBACK TITLES

ROMANCE

HISTORICAL

MEDICAL™

0910 Gen Std

MILLS & BOON®

OCTOBER 2010 LARGE PRINT TITLES

ROMANCE

HISTORICAL

MEDICAL™

Gen Std HB

MILLS & BOON

NOVEMBER 2010 HARDBACK TITLES

ROMANCE

The Dutiful Wife	Penny Jordan
His Christmas Virgin	Carole Mortimer
Public Marriage, Private Secrets	Helen Bianchin
Forbidden or For Bedding?	Julia James
The Twelve Nights of Christmas	Sarah Morgan
In Christofides' Keeping	Abby Green
The Italian's Blushing Gardener	Christina Hollis
The Socialite and the Cattle King	Lindsay Armstrong
Tabloid Affair, Secretly Pregnant!	Mira Lyn Kelly
Maharaja's Mistress	Susan Stephens
Christmas with her Boss	Marion Lennox
Firefighter's Doorstep Baby	Barbara McMahon
Daddy by Christmas	Patricia Thayer
Christmas Magic on the Mountain	Melissa McClone
A FAIRYTALE CHRISTMAS	Susan Meier & Barbara Wallace
The Soldier's Untamed Heart	Nikki Logan
Dr Zinetti's Snowkissed Bride	Sarah Morgan
The Christmas Baby Bump	Lynne Marshall

HISTORICAL

Courting Miss Vallois	Gail Whitiker
Reprobate Lord, Runaway Lady	Isabelle Goddard
The Bride Wore Scandal	Helen Dickson

MEDICAL™

Christmas in Bluebell Cove	Abigail Gordon
The Village Nurse's Happy-Ever-After	Abigail Gordon
The Most Magical Gift of All	Fiona Lowe
Christmas Miracle: A Family	Dianne Drake

MILLS & BOON

NOVEMBER 2010 LARGE PRINT TITLES

ROMANCE

HISTORICAL

MEDICAL™